STRUGGLER

Suhrita Das

BLUEROSE PUBLISHERS
India | U.K.

Copyright © Suhrita Das 2024

All rights reserved by author. No part of this publication may be reproduced, stored in a retrieval system or transmitted in any form or by any means, electronic, mechanical, photocopying, recording or otherwise, without the prior permission of the author. Although every precaution has been taken to verify the accuracy of the information contained herein, the publisher assumes no responsibility for any errors or omissions. No liability is assumed for damages that may result from the use of information contained within.

BlueRose Publishers takes no responsibility for any damages, losses, or liabilities that may arise from the use or misuse of the information, products, or services provided in this publication.

For permissions requests or inquiries regarding this publication, please contact:

BLUEROSE PUBLISHERS
www.BlueRoseONE.com
info@bluerosepublishers.com
+91 8882 898 898
+4407342408967

ISBN: 978-93-6261-934-1

Cover design: Rishav Rai
Typesetting: Rohit

First Edition: June 2024

Thank you

Children are the future we leave back in the world and it is our duty as elders to pass on everything we have gathered in our lives.. sorrow, joy, tears, beauty, love, despair all the seasons. To Misha and Gino without whom I couldn't have been a mother.

To Bhatt Saab without whose guiding light my dream of writing would have remained just a dream.

To our Writing Room full of talented, lyricists, writers, and tomorrow's film makers Shweta Bothra, Aman Puranik, Subham Dhiman, and Gino Sengupta who have churned the screenplay of the film over and over again.

To today's and tomorrow's brightest musicians Puneet Dixit Shagnik Kole and Aryan Tiwari.

Introduction

Struggler delves into the turbulent journey of Kabir, a young man torn between tradition and modernity, as he navigates the treacherous waters of the entertainment industry. Born into the mystical Baul tradition of Bengal, Kabir's father Pobon Das Baul staunchly believes in the diktats of the Bauls, where singing is an act of devotion rather than a pursuit of fame and fortune. However, Kabir rebels against his father's teachings and succumbs to the allure of fame, wealth, and power, fuelled by the insatiable status anxiety of the 21st century. As Kabir dives headfirst into the cutthroat world of Mumbai's entertainment scene, he finds himself ensnared in its dark underbelly of immorality and excess. Seduced by the promise of success, Kabir plunges into a whirlwind of drugs, hard sex, and moral compromise, losing himself in the hedonistic pursuit of pleasure and validation. Amidst the haze of vice and debauchery, Kabir's authenticity is gradually eroded, and he becomes a mere shadow of his former self. But amidst the chaos, there is a glimmer of hope in the form of Sofi, a woman who sees beyond Kabir's facade and recognizes the purity of his soul. Just as Kabir begins to claw his way out of the darkness with Sofi's help, tragedy strikes. He finds himself falsely accused of a murder he did not commit, trapped in a web of deceit and betrayal. Kabir must confront the consequences of his actions and fight to clear his name, all while grappling with the inner demons that threaten to consume him. Through Sofi's unwavering belief in Kabir's inherent goodness and the sacrifices she makes, including putting her own life on the line, Kabir finds the strength to confront his past and seek redemption. As he battles against the odds to prove his innocence, Kabir learns that true fulfillment lies not in the fleeting allure of fame and fortune but in reconnecting with his spiritual roots and embracing the essence of his Baul heritage. In the end, "Struggler" serves as a gritty and poignant exploration of the human condition, revealing the devastating consequences of unchecked ambition and the enduring power of love, sacrifice, redemption, and the pursuit of authenticity amidst the darkness of the modern world.

Mumbai city. The Sin city. The entertainment capital of India. It will be monsoon for another three months . As evening creeps in, the thick sheets of rain have slowed down to a gentle whisper like snowflakes kissing the earth. A man in a black snazzy shirt unbuttoned to leave his tanned, toned torso bare and thick silver rings hanging from his ear lobes, his bleached, curly hair flying loose in the wind drives through the wet streets of the city. He must be 28, with large, blazing eyes, he is Kabir. He rides past the alcohol shops littered with chauffeurs waiting to collect booze for the high and mighty, and a snail of guests waiting outside the sea food joints and coffee shops. Thin, wiry-framed men who work in construction sites, drive Ubers, and work as peons in large offices hailing from Bihar, Madhya Pradesh, Orissa, West Bengal with their families and children race towards the Juhu Beach like the ocean was throwing up gold. These are all signs of an early Friday evening bringing in a lazy weekend.

The giant hoarding at the Juhu Tara Rd. crossing has changed from iPhone 14 to the latest iPhone15 this week. Right beneath the sophisticated hoarding stand, rickety children in tattered clothes and potted bellies holding large balloons with blue, violet, and green lights blinking inside of them. Thirty Rupees each. For every balloon sold they make Three Rupees. Women in rags sit with bunches of roses in red, peach, and white brought back from church services and cemeteries. They carefully remove the withering petals on the outer rims of each flower to make them fresh and new again for selling in bunches when the traffic comes to a halt. Thin girls in their teen's sport neon bras and flaming orange lipsticks and clothes bought from the Bandra fashion street wait patiently to catch the eye of a rich customer who would take them away to Lonavla or Alibaug and give them a sturdy weekend income. And the vibrant family of the poker-marked street dancer thrives in another corner. The man in his bare chest and thick coiled hair has his forehead and face, the pits on his nose and cheeks are all marked with yellow dots, and his eye lids are painted red. He wraps the sturdy, dirty whip again and again against his bronze back while his wife begs and his children watch him while chewing dry Paav a generous pedestrian must have thrown at them. Kabir is a co-traveler with each one of them in this gigantic city, they throb in his being and call out to whisper a lullaby, "You too, soon will stink like us, and look and feel wretched, you will drop out by the sidewalk of this large, impersonal city... anytime now".

He is jolted out of his deep moments of reflection as he hears the sounds of car honks. They are roaring, calling out to him, asking him for speeding up his pace. Life on the high street isn't slow or easy. They are the weekenders, drunk, thrill-seeking, and rolling out of expensive cars. Their earlier generations have worked through blood and sweat to push all of this into their hands! And then the roar of his Harley Davidson racing past the mud slush on the black cobalt road. This is his only excitement, the ride on this machine. It's a part of his being, like a limb he has learned to maneuver over time and almost hears it speak back to him. While the city whacks him every day and reminds him he hasn't made it, this ride on his mean machine makes him feel alive and okay- Kabir like a bird taking off on a full flight. And above all the honking and yelling as his bike maneuvers itself around Juhu Tara Road a tune is born in his chest. Kabir, a restless child of music is not willing to give up on himself. Though waiting impatiently in the wings of Mumbai for five years now he begins to whistle lightly. Tunes have a way with him, they find him in those corners, crevices when he is hitting the rock bottom of his loneliness.

But his faint tune soon gets drowned in the urgency of making a living in the demanding cosmopolitan. The machine takes a turn to enter the humongous Marriott hotel in Juhu. The entrance is chock-a-block with plush cars restlessly waiting to enter at this hour. The Hotel rooms will be bustling with families, illicit lovers, escorts (dressed like starlets) entertaining difficult customers, and the restaurants throwing in some new food fairs. Kabir slides through the back gate to park his bike and quickly races into the staff section. The ticking clock in his head now gets louder. He is already late, by three minutes.

Once inside the locker room, Kabir takes off his helmet and opens his locker. His locker is a storehouse of stickers. Guns n Roses, Metallica, the Eagles, and small memory items he hasn't lost over the years. Like his dream of making it as a singer. A little plastic car with tiny doors opening on either side sits on the shelf above his electric guitar. He bought it when he was four, he went with his father Pobon Das Baul to one of the fairs in their village named Dhulishor somewhere in the innards of Bengal. Pobon wanted to gift his child a small Dotara, and Kabir chose the car. And a jacket stares at him, a leather one which each time he dons he is on top of the world.

As Kabir touches the tiny faded red car his ears pick up a faint sound. A whimpering, soft cry. And it is at this very moment that the loudspeaker in the locker room crackles and comes alive. It blares with the voice of the thin and tall Sandeep the coffee shop manager. "Calling Singer Kabir and team..Singer Kabir?" Kabir is about to pick the guitar gently out of the locker room and slide out. But that whimper? That gentle cry? Is someone calling for help? In this cutthroat, deal-making city where no one has time for anyone Kabir cannot stop himself. Though he knows Sandeep will be ugly and full of slang Kabir rushes in the direction of the array of toilets.

The whimper is louder now. He comes in front of the stall where he sees a shadow pouring out from beneath the door. He gently taps, and the whimper stops. He taps again, now louder, almost thumping. Kabir's heart tells him someone needs help inside. He brings his arm and body to bang enough to throw the light door apart. Inside sits the large, tall, and thick-built Anthony D'Souza with a sharp carving knife. His bare, white skin on his wrist is visible as he has folded up his white, crisp shirt waiting to run the carving knife through it. Kabir plunges to take away the knife, a scuffle ensues as D'souza is not willing to let it go. Kabir puts in all his might but D Souza is heavily built and has all the strength in his arms. A sharp cut slits through Kabir'a palm. The raw pain throbs in his nerves, blood oozes dripping on D Souza's pristine white shirt while Sandeep on the loudspeaker keeps calling out for Kabir like it were not a name but a slang. With a little more struggle Kabir manages to disarm the burly, large-built senior Chef. The minute D'Souza lets go of the knife Kabir holds him close and gently pulls out the beautiful aging man from the tiny toilet. He holds his wound under the cold running water of the basin while he keeps his vigilant eyes on the elderly man who has slumped on a weathered sofa kept in a corner.

D'Souza cries aloud with a sense of defeat and then with great difficulty he picks himself up to start the tap at another basin and splashes the cold water on his sweating, grimy face. "Why Chef?" asks Kabir while getting into his leather jacket and pulling up his guitar. Kabir is a few steps away from the hotel coffee shop and he knows what awaits him for reporting ten minutes late.

D'souza takes out his phone and shows Kabir the news clip he's been haunted by since the morning. On the phone screen flashes an old photograph of a young girl in a sequined dress and thick, flowing hair. It's Jenny, D'Souza's daughter who always wanted to be an actress. As Kabir scrolls down to the news the older man cries softly, "Everything I had I put into her grooming and well-being Kabir! And the stupid girl takes the offer of some shady Production and lands up in Dubai to be told that she is carrying cocaine with her inside the art piece they have handed over to her minutes before boarding the flight? Who will believe the truth that the fucking trophy was given to her by the same production house that has no existence in Dubai? I don't have money to pay a lawyer and prevent her from getting into prison for fourteen years, I don't know how to avoid every questioning face that asks if my daughter is indeed a drug dealer? I should die, Kabir, for God I have no answers, I deserve to...I need to die." Kabir feels a lump in his throat, a need to reach out to this ageing man whom he has known for the past two months since he signed in the coffee shop. He wraps a thick napkin around his palm and then hugs him dearly, calling out, "No Anthony, death is not the answer you are looking for. We will do something about this, we will." D'Souza holds the boy in his heavy arms awkwardly for a while and then lets go, "Look at your palm man, it must be hurting. Now go make a living in this ugly city young man. You've made me live now...another fucking twenty years, you bastard." Kabir smiles to that, winks at the old chef, and picks up his guitar to float into the coffee shop.

The weekend crowd is just beginning to fill up the tables. The coffee shop has set up elaborate counters of seafood, raw meat, chaats, and vegetables, and as guests begin to line up with their plates Sandeep in his starched coat and gelled-back hair races towards Kabir who by now has climbed up to the platform looking over the coffee shop and begins to tune his guitar. He comes close to Kabir's ear and whispers with an ugly smile on his face while blocking the mike with his hand, "Madarchod, is this your grandfather's hotel where you can walk in any time you wish, and start strumming the bloody guitar?" Kabir has no words to give back while he tunes his guitar. Sandeep's cussing persists, they make Kabir's skin ruddy, and bare, something raw in his centre is churning, coming alive. An animal whose leaping out he fears.

Sandeep now notices the fresh wound in Kabir's palm, blood still trickles down despite a thick white napkin tied around it. "And what is this? Did you have a street fight? I cannot allow criminals to sing and entertain in my hotel." Kabir gives it back to Sandeep, "No, I was just trying to save your senior chef who would have killed himself, his daughter..." Sandeep silences Kabir with an ugly expression, "Haa haa his hot-headed daughter caught with drugs on her. His end is anyhow here, you save your back now!" Kabir stays silent as he gets into the beat of the song he is going to sing. It is clear and throbbing in his head from dawn. His own written and composed "Teen jahaan ka malik tu Khuda..tere dil ko dayaa kyu nahi aata" (Almighty you are the creator of the three worlds and yet you are heartless to watch it all..) the strumming of the chords, the tune tells Sandip where it is going, "You are playing one of those again haa? Your stuff?" Kabir nods and then bringing the mike close to him rolls it out in his thunderous voice. The song has been haunting him. His father's kind, aged face visits him as if he were blessing him from miles across, from the red, sodden earth of Dhulishor whose smell visits Kabir every night. Pobon will always remain Kabir's Guru. It is humming Pobon's tunes from childhood that made Kabir find his tunes and words. One fine day when he found his songs to sing Kabir rushed to sing them to Pobon, the man stared at the young boy unable to understand them, nodded, and walked away. The tunes never left Kabir, they were his. He had a gift and only he knew that. Everyone has a gift. He had learned this from his Baba but he rejected Kabir's tunes as transient, flippant.

The guests heap their plates with crab claws and fill their glasses with more wine, Kabir sings on amidst the clitter clatter of plates and forks, mindless merry-making and backbiting. Sandeep now standing near one of the live counters eyes Kabir, wanting him to sing some popular hits of Bollywood next. Kabir holds his ground, it's not a Bar in Malad or Goregaon he is singing in, these are people who listen to music and have grown a taste of their own. They have the ear for an original if they hear one. Who knows, maybe the weekend wave will bring in a Producer, a music label honcho? As Kabir ends "Teen Duniya" and bows to the claps his eyes travel to a corner table down below. A tall, well-built man surely into his 50s sits with a drink. His hair, salt and pepper, gelled back like a gangster in an American film. With him is a woman. Must be a few years younger than Kabir? Salt and Pepper and she seem to be a couple. It is her large, lit-up eyes that draw him, she is staring back at him oddly too. Her eyes are glazed, like she where under the influence of something. Kabir strums the guitar, his heart goes to the next number he loves the most, "Chal kahi gum ho jaaye hum dono" (let us lose ourselves to the unknown). As the tune and words roll out Kabir continues to keep his gaze fixed on her, Smouldering Eyes. He'd just named her that under his breath.

While she is drawn into the song fully Salt n Pepper is constantly attending to phone calls, he looks ill-tempered, loud, a bully. She is still, keeping her contact with Kabir knowing the contact is reaching him and making him sing from his core. And just then suddenly Salt n Pepper snaps at her observing that her drink remains untouched. He is talking down to her, leaving her a little ashamed of herself, the guests at the tables near them look back, he cares a fuck. She keeps her head low. Kabir wants her to stay a little longer, a little. But the grumpy Salt n Pepper, probably her husband, suddenly holds her arm and pulls her up. The others conscious of having wanted to witness this drama now go back to their eating and merry-making aware of being voyeurs. He is shouting at her, she looks scared. Kabir continues to sing. The man pulls her through the orchard of tables and on his way out throws a stash of Rupees at Sandeep.

A few seconds pass by, and all that stares back at Kabir is the vacant table. Her glass with a hint of her lipstick on it. A lifeless, crumpled napkin. He tries to engage with the chair she was on a few seconds ago to still sing with his spirits high. But his heart is hit by a sudden void he never knew of before this moment. Like a thorn stuck in his neck, now softly oozing blood. The raw pain on his palm has disappeared in comparison to this. One moment, a flash, in a city where faces, and people appear and disappear like changing phases of the moon and yet it felt so..so real to him. Her face was at the dark end of the room, illumined slightly by a thick candle on the table. He gives up this false attempt, he stops singing. The crowd has got busier with the live counters steaming, sizzling with lobsters and squids, someone cooking up pasta, and someone baking a pizza made to order.

He keeps his guitar aside and walks up towards the stacked plates. His brain is bursting now with the sounds of cheer, plans for the two days ahead, business plans for the year ahead, babies crank and wanting to be let out of their stuffy prams. This is why they earn and work so hard. To plan, keep at it, planning. Every Friday, every month, every year the same plan for the cycle of earn, buy, spend, and earn again. Kabir is fascinated by this cycle as he walks through the sea of tables. He quickly comes to the non-veg counter picks up a plate and piles a lot of chicken biriyani on it. The creamy, buttery smell of it, the saffron and the chunks of meat are calling him. He can't remember when he ate his last meal. As he picks a fork and moves in the direction of the table where she was seated minutes ago Kabir spots Sandeep walking up to him with a visible rage in his body. Kabir has lifted a chunk of soft meat with a little rice to bring to his mouth when Sandeep roughly comes up to pick Kabir's plate. Kabir promptly keeps the fork and holds the plate back from his side. While the diners are inquiring about the kebabs or Naans they asked for while on the go they are alarmed by this new drama unfolding. Quite a dinner this day. Kabir continues to gaze at Sandeep while retaining the pull at the plate from his side. Sandeep bends and guzzles out in a slithering voice, "Who told you to pick up a fucking plate and start feasting?" Kabir holds the plate rightfully, it is a part of his payment. "I say let it go, why did you stop singing? Do you know what your job is? It is to entertain my guests, not to become one of them. Why the fuck are you here? To get me more guests." Kabir can see more heads flip, and more walking steps stop. By now the entire coffee shop has come to a standstill, the services at the live counters and the waiters frozen in mid-action. The clitter-clatter of the plates and forks has died down. Sandeep blares like a mad bull spouting an ugly anger that is more towards himself perhaps. Years ago he must have landed here to start his own restaurant from Ludhiana or Raebareli. While no funds arrived and no one showed up to give him the support, he never left. Instead. he adjusted to training as a manager and taking orders. He earns a living, but in Kabir's eyes, his songs remind Sandeep that he gave up on himself, and his dreams.

Kabir has now begun feeling the throb in his head, a tune that was forming since he had seen Smouldering Eyes was just beginning to acquire wings but now it is lost forever. His head is bursting, he can feel it, it is groping for the words, to climb a high. Sandeep is trying harder than ever before to snatch away the plate from his hand. By now Kabir's stomach is full of humiliation and the hunger has disappeared. His cheeks look flushed and his chest brimming with tears. As Sandeep pulls the plate with one large tug Kabir gently gets up from his chair and lets it go. Softly. Sandeep is left off balance not having been able to predict this and let go of Kabir. He balances his tight shoes and prevents the plate from slipping away but lands on the floor with the rice and meat over him. Slowly, softly and then the ceramic plate slides from his hand and lands on the floor neatly cracking into two half-moons and falling by his side. He stares at the pieces calculating the money he shall have to let them deduct from his salary for this.

The guests are still taken aback as they haven't seen this kind of drama in their lives, some of them already recording this, posting it live on their social media accounts. It's the stuff that television serials are made of, the stuff that people in the lower classes of life live on. Kabir walks away letting the tears roll down, but he walks away with his head held high, his heart rushed with the memory of a man he hasn't seen for five years now but every single day he quietly remembers him, prays for him and awaits a day when they will hug again dearly. Pobon Das's gentle face flashes on Kabir's phone screen as he checks a status update someone has put up on social media. Pobon is singing in a concert put together for him in Paris. With raised hands, he calls out to the Gods, his Dotaara strumming, his voice thundering in the French air. Does he miss Kabir? As he misses his mystic father? Kabir keeps his phone back and races out into the night air.

The outside is glowing and blaring with a Baarati making an entrance into the hotel premises. "Aaj mere yaar ki shaadi hai" being played on all kinds of instruments cracks through the walls of the large, plush building. Kabir wipes his tears as he glides past the premises. His phone is ringing incessantly in his pocket. He rides away a little further from the hotel, where the lights are a little dim, and a narrow lane leads to the beach. Kabir parks his Harley Davidson with the utmost care, he then takes off his helmet and finally answers the call. She sounds a little high. Anu Mahajan, his lover cum manager. A decade older than him, Anu has been in the business of talent hunting since the time they rejected her as the first lead in Hindi films.

"Where the fuck have you been all evening?" she asks, taking a long drag of her cigarette. Kabir is silent, gauging her mood. Is this one of her black moods? Will she burst into slang, and begin throwing things around her, or has she already plundered her well done-up apartment? Did the supply boy, rickety Jolly Jadav bring her a new stock of MD and is she high on it? Kabir stutters while walking a little away from the bike, looking at the sea now turbulent and roaring, he must lie with a flare and soothe her. He begins softly, "Anu I am somewhere near my home, I have been sleeping all day. was feeling.." He can feel the temperature in her breath rise, she is like a snake ready to strike. Anu snarls back at him, "Kabir my agency is ten years old today. Do you know what it takes to be for ten years on the racing track? Any fucking racing track for that matter? All my models, starlets, managers, and everyone who Anu Mahajan represents and has given work to in this narrow-minded, perception-creating business is here! Celebrating, drinking champagne, and eating Sushi. *Saala Madarchod (dumb motherfucker)*, where are you? My biggest asset? Most promising are you and you arrogant bastard choose to sleep it off?" Anu is waiting for an answer. Kabir has known her for five years now, she can be lied to or be told the truth but you cannot remain limp or silent. Anu calls for participation, she needs an answer.

Kabir begins again, "Anu I am sorry, I will come to you now, I am on my way actually, am close." Kabir knows the traffic will be sticky around Anu's house in Bandra, he can't reach before half an hour, and yet he continues to speak. She is silent, sounds of loose cheer, and drunk repartee flow in from the other end of the phone. Kabir nervously calls out, "Anu? Are you there?" there's still no response. She is clicking away on her other phone, and one of her boys has sent screenshots of Kabir entering the Marriott and leaving after two hours. As she sees them she throws away her cigarette and blares, "Yes I am fucking right here! I am there to be backstabbed each time, every time." Kabir's stomach drops, his animal instinct tells him she's found out. She continues, "So you have been singing in the Marriott like some Christmas carol singer and you thought I would never come to know?" Silence throbs between them. Anu rages again, " Is this where I should place my trust? How much do they pay you? What is it that they are giving away Kabir that I didn't give you?" Anu silences and transpires a feeling of being deeply hurt. He knows he has to go there, and explain to her everything. He's messed it up again. Now no matter what it takes, he has to make it up to her.

Kabir makes a blinding race riding past the cars and autorickshaws at maddening speed. The shortcuts are like the back of his hands, he glides through them to reach as fast as he can. Even the by-lanes are screaming with people and cars. While Kabir is stranded in a narrow lane near the Bandra fashion street and a thousand horns honk back and forth, he is shot into the memory of that afternoon when Anu came home. He had sung with his Baba at the 'Baul Sammelon' of Dhulishor. He assisted his Baba all night in the background only filling in for him when he sipped water or changed from one *Alkhalla* (patch-work robe) to another. And then at Two in the morning when his Baba had strummed the Dotaara for the last time and sung his biggest hit, *"Milon hobe koto diney..amar moner manusher o shoney"* (when will I meet the one I yearn to meet, my only beloved) and called it a day the lights on the tiny stage went off. The crowd dispersed but in no time the old were replaced by the young. And from behind the curtain came a Kabir with his hair wet and pushed back, sporting one rare red jacket his father didn't know about and he sang cracking into the dawn. One song after another from Hindi films.

Two of the Heads of the village Amulya and Ranjit heard about Anu who was sifting corner to corner of the country looking for talent. She was bringing talent for the latest Indian Talent Hunt show, every singer meant an additional commission for her, and she was offering a lumpsum to every local person who led her to a true and rare talent. Anu had the ears of a music connoisseur, and the eyes of a hawk. She sat down in the crowd, wrapped in a black shawl, choosing to stay anonymous. She wanted to know if this boy was indeed what

Amulya and Ranjit had promised. At dawn she got up and matched eyes with them as they had promised her, once she set her eyes on Kabir, she would not look away from him. She approved of Kabir and acknowledged their contribution. Only when Anu gave the stacks of 500 Rupees to Amulya and Ranjit did they show them the way to Pobon Das Baul's hut.

Anu was direct and spoke straight to Kabir knowing he was the boy whose hunger had moved her. She mentioned a five-year contract, singing opportunity in multiple talent shows, and exposure to music professionals in the film industry to groom himself. And of course, money, lifestyle. Kabir did not understand clearly what those perks meant and yet he knew Anu could mean a new life for him. Deep in his heart, Kabir knew he deserved all that and more; much more, a limitless more than millions and millions of youngsters in this country hailing from villages and towns think they deserve.

That was the beginning of Kabir's life. He rushed to Pobon who was grooming young children in his large and open room and shared the good news with him. The aged musician whose eyes had seen beyond his years, took a look at Anu and brought back Kabir to the other room. He closed the door of the hut and slapped Kabir. The ripe man of the world knew the boy was being led into his weak self, temptations, and desires of the big and bad world. He couldn't think of Kabir being lost in the concrete jungle of a thousand look-alikes! But it was the first time that Kabir saw beyond his Baba, he wanted to. In a huff then he picked a couple of worn-out t-shirts, a pair of trousers, and his book of songs. He put everything into a large cloth bag, opened the doors of the hut, and stepped out to join Anu. As they walked away in the direction of a gleaming SUV Pobon shouted wailing alone in his hut, "The city will swallow you, my child, it will rid you of your soul and make you a crawling worm. You will never be able to sing again." Pobon's curse still haunts the innards of Kabir as he enters Anu's building.

The guard Tiwari gives him a sturdy salute and calls out, *"Party.. party chaalu hai !! Aap kahaa reh gaye?"* (there's a party going on, why are you going only now?). Kabir ignores him, parks his bike in his allotted place, and takes the lift.

Anu's apartment announces itself even before her tall, thickly carved metallic door opens. There are plants in ceramic pots of various colours, shapes, and sizes that thrive, cactus mostly. A large, antique metal bell she picked up from Kashmir hangs awaiting being rung and a large Diyaa picked up from craftsmen in Tanjore welcoming on the way. The wall is full of black and white photographs of Hollywood stars and studios. Kabir hesitantly rings the doorbell. The sounds inside are softer now. A few seconds pass by, no response. And then Anaika one of Anu's top models, a little sloshed, with red antlers adorning her head opens the door. She bends in the correct angle giving Kabir a view of her fair cleavage. Kabir stays fixed on her eyes and asks, "Anu? Please tell her.." Anu calls out from behind, "Come in Kabir!" Anaika gives a mischievous smile and moves aside provoking Kabir to brush past her well-pronounced , bulbous butt. He pushes her away gently holding her by her arm and then enters. Anu is seated amidst a heap of used wine glasses, beer bottles, and a cake that has eaten its way into the last layer. She continues to gaze at her whiskey glass. She calls out, "Go to our room, I will say bye to everyone leaving and come to you."

Without waiting for a second Kabir walks away. Anu's bedroom is cold, and dark, with a strange lamp at the bedside flashing a purple, pink, and blue light from time to time. A large painting hangs above her bed, a copy of Frida Kahlo's self-portrait. Kabir sits on the large chair kept beside the window. The road beneath is deserted but for an occasional car or youngsters walking in groups. Assistants, and technicians creep out of Mehboob studio for a late plate of steaming Biriyani at Lucky Restuarant. Kabir can feel his heart beating loudly in his chest. He is eager and anxious to meet Anu and explain everything to her, he is hoping things return to normalcy between them like before. As he settles on the long antique chair Kabir's eyes droop, slumber almost pulling him down. The sweet scent Anu uses for her bedroom is a great seduction. After almost half an hour Kabir can hear the last Byes, Ciaos, and See Yaa's and the main metallic door shuts with Anu putting the multiple locks in place. It tightens something in Kabir's chest.

As if, a cruel, ugly jealous rage were walking towards him, a side of hers she hadn't revealed until now. A minute or so later having turned off the lights outside Anu creeps in and closes the door behind her. She removes her silken gown at the door and steps forward in the direction of Kabir. The relief is she is not mad at him, but drunk. Anu comes up to him and begins to unbutton his shirt. "Why have you not got this stinking shirt off your skin and why are you not waiting to pounce on me? Why are you making me undress you? As if it were our first time..you know our drill right?" Kabir lets Anu dig her nails into his chest each time she unbuttons him, every pore in his body saying no. His insides are barking for help, he wants to be heard, it's not one of those days, one of those nights. Even before he can say something Anu who has a certain way of exercising her force on him throws him on her large bed. Kabir lays in the darkness, naked, and cold with his head throbbing in pain, this is exactly when a flash of Smouldering Eyes from the Marriott coffee shop visits him. While Sandeep harassed him, while the plate cracked and Kabir walked away to never look back despite his bank account dwindling her gaze pierced him and drilled his insides. He remembers every detail of hers most fiercely, even if from a distance. Who was she? Why did he feel like for a few seconds all the people had disappeared leaving only him singing to her? By now Anu has pulled his hands to let them cradle her large breasts, a technique, a skill she has taught him for years. It arouses her quick and deep. While she is waiting for something to start between them, a spark a lash and the unfolding of an engaging sensuous night, Kabir lays still. Not a fiber in his body making an effort to make her feel ..he is in.

Now Anu piles up her tall, broad body on him, holding him with her thighs tight, engaging roughly. He pleads, "Anu, not tonight? Let's not? Please?" Anu brings her mouth reeking of vodka and whiskey close to his mouth and bites him hard on his lips. A tear from Kabir's left eye falls by. The night ticks away until dawn Anu needs to rest and sleep until the evening when she has to look over a publicity event in BKC. Kabir picks himself up, a large digital clock says it's Five in the morning. As Kabir fumbles in the dark looking for his shirt and denim the unspoken words remain in him. Anu raises her long, lithe hand to touch Kabir's chest and make him aware that she realizes he is going. Within Kabir starts the vicious cycle of fear, another day, another same fucking day of nothingness. Even the

Marriott is gone from his fold now. Maybe he should ask Sunny a struggling sound recordist from Bodhgaya for another opening in some Bar or Café in Andheri West. His head is ticking, Kabir knows he has to tell Anu what he needs to tell him now or never.

He calls out gently, "Can I tell you something? Please will you listen to me?" Anu raises her long neck to reach out for her silver cigarette box. She takes out a tall, slim one and grips it between her chapped lips, the remains of last night's bright red pigments still rubbing off on the white surface of the cigarette. She looks at Kabir expecting him to pick up the lighter and set it alight. She is fond of Kabir, she saw him that night in Dhulishor and knew there was something indeed rare and precious in the boy, but she didn't want to give him away, she wanted to groom, smother, and spoil him so he'd want all the things she could provide him more and more. That way Kabir would never want to touch the hunger and uncertainty of needing to become a singer, he would always be on his toes with her demands. Always lighting her cigarettes! As he lights her cigarette and keeps away the lighter, Anu finally asks taking in her first, hard puff of the day, " What my darling K?" Kabir holds himself together and finally says the words, "Anu it's been five years."

Anu in a second knows where this is coming from and where this could go. She has been a sharp, crude deal maker in the deal city for a decade and more, she knows it's time to claim who belongs where or the deal could slip out of her long, artistic fingers. "So?" as if a little puzzled she waits for him to answer knowing how his cycles work. Kabir now speaks out for himself once and for all, "I don't want to stay here and keep doing this anymore. This is not why I came here." He gets up to come close to Anu's side of the bed and , holds her other hand. "Please Anu, say I don't have it in me and I will go back, but you have just kept me guarded and given me shows here and there, I haven't auditioned for once or even tried anyone else. I wanted them to hear my voice, I wanted to be heard, Anu. It won't happen ever, I don't know anyone apart from you in this city or this music world. Let me go. Please?" In a second Anu sits up, knowing she must take charge and get a little bare with her puppy. She will fight like a bitch on the streets for her bone, not taking any shit lying down. She flares up, "Oh so now Mister Talented thinks he is absolutely in charge and can take a call for himself? You are no one to take that call, Mister, I have invested in you, groomed you all these years, taught you to dress up, sit, talk, speak like this!" the words in Kabir's head are louder now, "And passed me around in your circle of business associates? Never introduced me to a Music Producer or Director to make them hear my voice! I did not come for this! I am leaving."

Kabir knows it's now or never. Maybe she will ask him to leave back the keys to the Harley Davidson, maybe she will ask him to move out of the flat, ask him to never come to her again. Maybe. But he has to step back and walk out, opening her large, thick metallic door, and never looking back. Leaving back the Harley Davidson which has been his drug, his pet, and his partner will hurt him truly. But it's better. He begins to walk away when Anu like a python hungry for days knows exactly when to go for the kill, when to thrust the diabolical bite. Anu throws herself on Kabir from behind him. She holds him tight in his grip, talking softly into his ear. "You are not going anywhere Mister; I will not let you cancel out on all my hard work. Wait, just fucking wait here." Having stopped Kabir in his tracks Anu walks back to her bedside desk and takes out something.

She throws a visiting card at Kabir and a stack of raw Two thousand Rupees notes. "Take that goddamn address and go talk to someone in Star Studio. I thought you liked all this we have between us more than anything else. Partying, being with me and my special friends, eating, drinking, being merry?? But you are waiting, waiting to be told to leave or stop singing or something. So go, go and get the rejection written all over your body, I am here to mother you back to life!" Kabir stares in disbelief at the visiting card. He has heard the name of this music director several times earlier, Darshan Taloja. His recent hits with Subham Acharya, the current singing sensation is a sure shot entry into the arena. Kabir steps forward to try and hug Anu. "Am sorry, sorry Anu, I should have been clearer about what I want, you were always there." Anu not impressed by Kabir's cautious gesture pushes him back and goes back to her bed sounding sleepy, "Close the door well behind when you leave and call in the evening only." Kabir can't wait for another second, now he can't wait for the day to ripen. The phone number of Darshan Taloja stares back at him, an impatient Kabir scolds himself saying it's not right to call anyone that important before Ten in the morning. His fingers type the number from the visiting card on his phone as the elevator glides down. He saves the number and restlessly wonders if dropping in a message this early would be good with a Namaste emoticon.

The morning air is cool, salty, and free of dust grains that otherwise float in the air continuously like snowflakes floating in the scenes of Dr. Zhivago. As Kabir drives, he takes in a deep breath to feel the day breaking in. In his head, he keeps saying aloud, "today is the first day of my life, it only is beginning to happen now, today is...". He snails through the traffic along with school buses, airport passengers, and supply vans to slowly journey back from the church bell tolling, the gothic and graffiti-laden world of Bandra to the mediocre, crammed, loud corners of Andheri. His eyes droop in tiredness and sleep, and yet again Smouldering Eyes visit him. Who was she? Will he ever see her again? So many faces, the seamless crowd in this city, expressions, and yet a pair of eyes stand out. Glistening, flowing towards him like a river of mirage in the desert.

Kabir keeps his eyes wide as much as he can. The Juhu Beach area is getting busy with morning walkers, joggers, yoga enthusiasts and tourists. He makes his way to the broken streets of Fun Republic through Veera Desai Rd. At the end of the road, behind a monstrous construction site, commanding a tiny portion of land and sky stands a thin, tall, weathered building. Kadam Chawl. Kabir turns off his bike and cautiously brings it down the broken, muddy road, which is primarily now a route for the bricks, the sand the cement to be carried in heavy lorries and for cranes to make way for the thirty-floor concrete giant coming up to overshadow the 'gharibon ki basti' (home for the destitute) Kadam Chawl. As Kabir neatly parks his bike and covers it well, he is caught by the flow of people going out of the building at this hour. Youngsters who work in departmental stores, stand for hours at makeup counters, part-time bar tenders cum receptionists, and the aged lot who despite their retirement spend their experience or knowledge in some office and still generate an income. As Kabir makes his way into the building, he greets, and salutes each of the young boys who run an all-night Chinese restaurant. Haara a thin boy in his weathered t-shirt and shorts whom Kabir helped come from Dhulishor races in his direction with a hot box stuffed with chow mein.

Kabir fishes into his pocket for a few currencies but the boys never take money from him. A year back he loaned money from Anu to help them make this food joint. The surrounding area is filled with studios where technicians edit, record, and shoot all night, this made their Chinese delivery already a hit! Kabir pats Haara gently on his head and walks in the direction of the lift. It's a long wait before the slow lift climbs down bringing more people to flush out of the building. After a few minutes the lift doors finally open. A couple of spot boys flush out, and an elderly woman with a hairless street dog steps out. At the sight of Kabir, Tanvi the aging actress bursts into joy. "Haven't seen you in three-four days my Jaan, so busy?" As she speaks her hairless pet Alien comes up to Kabir wagging his tail seeking love. Kabir bends down to hug the lost, sad dog. He calls out without matching his eyes with Tanvi, "*Haan my heroine*, auditioning for lead singer back-to-back!!" Tanvi quietly observes him loving the hairless Alien and the animal responding haplessly. Her eyes have seen years in the ever-changing entertainment industry where it all might add up to something and then be taken away from you in moments by someone younger, smarter, and more astute in selling oneself. She decides to leave it at that. She calls out, "*Oh Kabir*, there's someplace in the world where to love and be loved you don't have to use words!" he gets up and keeping his head lowered gets into the lift, "See you, Heroine." Tanvi walks away gallantly in her garish costume of her last hit film from the early 80s, "Jaanbaaz" with Alien by her side. The lift doors close leaving Kabir in his resounding silence.

Kabir lives on the thirteenth floor. Many times, before he can reach home the lift doors open and shut. People emerge, walk in and look at each other. Smells of talcum powder, cheap body sprays, herbal hair oil mix and merge. People leave, and their smells linger. Kabir patiently waits for his turn to step out. Finally, he does that and when he does so his phone begins to ring. He looks at the toll-free number with a strange large diamond sparkling in the middle of the screen. Kabir picks it up. A voice floats in, "Your future is not for you to wait, it is for you to live. Live it now. You have talent, we have opportunities, come join hands let's shape the future. Diamond Music!!" Kabir stares at it for a while then blocks the number. He enters home, despite the persisting thick darkness chinks of light tear in past the expensive, thick curtains he's put up. Enough light to see the large photograph of Pobon that he has placed at the entrance way. He touches it with both his hands and rests his forehead on the cold glass. The silence hits him, the loneliness waiting at the end of the journey. While the world is waking up to a new day, bundles of possibilities, Kabir must call it a day.

He quickly changes into a track pant and t-shirt and places the box of noodles that Haara gave on the marble slab, telling himself he will eat when he is up. As he rubs off the grime and dust from his face Sandeep's words climb on him, but Anu is kind, and generous. He is going to start his life now. As Kabir settles with the ac freezing and the blanket pulled up to finally close his eyes, within seconds the doorbell rings. No one comes at this hour. The garbage girl Lakshmi from Haryana does not bother Kabir, and neither do the Pav sellers or other vendors. The bell keeps ringing. He finally gets out of his cot to open the door.

What stands in front of him is a strange figure. Slithering like a snake, glowing with lights fitted around her body, a tall, able-bodied, fully made-up from head to toe like a danseuse etched in the temples of south India. A transgender. A low tune of a snake charmer plays, it almost emits from her body. As Kabir stands at his doorstep the regular garbage collection from doors happens, the children are being taken to school, the elders step out, and as life flows as usual the transgender twirls and makes her curvaceous moves of some kind of a Naagin dance in rhythm with the music. After a few seconds, she comes to a still and holds herself in a pose with her arms raised in a Namaste while catching her breath. Kabir brings out his wallet and takes out a Rs 100 note.

As he produces it expecting the transgender to take it and leave, she holds his hand and pushes it away. "I did not come for this, is this what you think of me?" Kabir is dumbstruck unable to gauge what is about to come next. She takes out a visiting card from a fold of her silken saree wound like a dhoti draping her entire body. Kabir brings it close to himself, it has the same logo as the anonymous calls he's been receiving for the past few weeks. "We will change your fate, your destiny Babuji, just join hands with us. I am the agent of Diamond

Music. The biggest company in our country that sells petrol, gas, medicines, and aerated drinks is now venturing into music. New voices, new tunes, new world, new India! Aren't you going to be a part of this Babuji?" Kabir returns the visiting card gently to her, she joins her hands, does a Pranaam, and concludes, "I am yours truly, Junior Siridevi". Kabir knows what he has to say, "You can be anybody, but I don't need this opportunity. Please take this and leave." He insists upon the hundred rupees note be taken by her. Suddenly another being, like an angered hyena flares up from the so long charming, blazing person.

"Don't need? Did you say you don't need help? Really? You will regret these words of yours, let me tell you. I can see the future with these very eyes of mine, there's doom waiting for you. Doom ...doom." Kabir now steps back and tries to close the door on her knowing this is not a person who deserves his time or kindness, he needs sleep, not these histrionics. Just as he closes the door Junior Siridevi steps in and holds the door with all her might and force, "Keep this card, God had come knocking on your door. You will call me. Know this, you will." With this, she throws the visiting card at Kabir and walks away turning on her music and lights and slithering away in the same snakish gait.

Kabir stares at the card, then gently closes the door and pushes the entire episode along with the visiting card into a corner of his mind to fall asleep. The large construction site has by now come fully alive, gnarling, roaring grinding away its teeth and fuming dust. Kabir has lost the window of sleep when it's still silent before the sounds begin. Some children play in his corridor getting a little time before their day school and Alien growls at them. Kabir's body floats into a lost land of tire, toil, memories, and a tune trying to hold on to him. And Smouldering Eyes, he will never see her again in this large, dusty, noisy town of wannabes. Never. This is why no one connects with anyone; the longevity of the transaction decides the depth and pursuit. Kabir must resist those eyes.

At Five in the evening, Kabir's phone rings aloud. He gets up quickly wondering if it is THE Darshan Taloja. It's an unknown number, maybe it's him. Kabir picks up and nervously calls out, "Hello?" A beat or two of silence follows in which Kabir can only hear his own heartbeat while the construction site continues to roar in the backdrop. Finally, the voice surfaces, "It's me, Sofi. I heard you singing in the Mariott yesterday?" Kabir hears the grains of her voice more closely now. Yes, it's indeed her, Smouldering Eyes. He stays silent as no words are surfacing in his consciousness. She continues, "Will you sing me the rest of the song, please? I am waiting for you in Juhu Beach. I could only manage your phone number and about an hour for myself. I am at the remote end of the beach, where a dark, smelly drainage river flows from the city into the ocean." The phone disconnects. Kabir is staring at the darkness, his heart beating with urgency as the one-hour time frame comes alive. A woman waiting on the beach for him to sing. He almost wanted to ask her why, why an hour only? He quickly throws cold water on his face, and gets into last night's shirt, and denims, his palm still hurting a little from the slash of D Souza's carving knife. He races out of the building in ten minutes knowing the lanes and by lanes where traffic will be less.

Kabir knows from her back, it's her. A woman staring at the sunset, the wind whipping up her hair not letting him see her face. He comes to stand close to her without speaking a word. She turns, knowing it's him. She points at the edgy rocks; they walk towards it. Kabir has Smouldering Eyes this close to him. Magic happens, this city that chews up and throws away people can also possibly make a connection carry on for so long. She too must have been left thirsting for him. Whom did she ask for his number? Sandeep? A secret good wish goes away for Sandeep from Kabir now! They climb onto a height and settle on the rocks. The daylights are dimming, the cricket match and the evening walkers and the stray dogs thrive. Kabir strums his guitar. The air is saline and warm, his song piercing her. He sings the middle, the end, and then the beginning again of '*Chal Kahi Gum Ho Jaaye*' not aware of her having climbed down a few layers. She is on her phone. He stops his singing. As she turns, she looks grave and distorted. Unrecognizable almost. Kabir thinks she will climb up to her and say what is going on. She calls out, "I have to go, Sorry. See you soon!" She begins to climb down to the beach and then walks away in the direction of Chowpatty. Kabir is dumbstruck by the taste of her gaze this close, her breath warm and welcoming. As she fades into the crowd Kabir gets up angry and empty making his way back to where he parked his bike. "Sofi" he calls out once to feel the sound of it in his mouth, he lets it float in his inner being.

Late in the evening, Darshan Taloja sends a message. Star Studio 10.30 am. Kabir's face lights up, he calls Anu to confirm the appointment. He asks her anxiously, "so will he give me a song or want me to sing one of mine? Is this a trial?" Anu silences the excited man who is like an imptient infant. Over and above the sound in her event at BKC she shouts from the wings "Darshan knows what he can get out of your voice. You be there and let him lead. Okay, Baba..." Kabir stares at his rack of clothes, his shoes, and his couple of perfume bottles. It's finally happening, a beginning, the curve, the turn has taken place. Then famished he quickly heats the stale chow that Haara gave him in a tub, picks a fork, and digs into it ravenously.

As Kabir eats he stares at the large photo of Pobon Das , he gets up to touch it with one hand and closes his eyes for a few moments. He can hear his Baba's voice, singing, shouting at him when he was a child, and that last day when he left. Here ends the turmoil, Kabir resolves to call him once he's sung the song in the studio. He kisses the photo and gets back to the oily chow mein knowing tomorrow will surely be the beginning of his new life.

By nine fifteen Kabir is out in the bustling, racing tracks of Mumbai City. Every possible road, every connector is dug up pushing normal rush hour delays to the unknown. This drive took him five years. He took out his bike, put on the helmet, and waved at Tanvi who sat in a corner of the premises taking out her flask of cheap whiskey and sipping into it from time to time. The Chinese food joint boys waved at him, the temple of Sainath around the corner of the lane tolled its bells as if for him.

Kabir rides away in the direction of Star Studio. 'Zindagi aa rahaa hu mein..' (life, here I come) he mutters under his breath. Once Kabir arrives at the red, large gates of Star Studio he observes the queue of strugglers lined along the boundary wall. A man with a strange placard stands nearby. On his placard is written, "Tree Man- Film looking for Producer. 21 days standing." He was there with them all these years, standing quietly for someone inside those plush cars gliding in and out of the studio to notice him. Anu never came to know. He never caught anyone's attention. Without letting his mind waver he now comes up to the security guard and shows them the gate pass Anu had sent over late at night. The guards look at each other, give a gentle nod, and let him in. As the red gates open Kabir feels a quick rush in his head. The pathway inside opens up to a series of buildings. A beautiful garden runs beside him, and a temple made of marble emitting Om Jai Jagdish Hare and thick perfumes of Agarbatti (incense sticks) stands tall.

Once he's parked his bike at the allotted corner Kabir checks his phone again for the exact building name where he is supposed to go. He tries calling Anu, an anticipation building in his chest, a fear of what's about to happen. Her number keeps ringing, too early for her to wake up if there's no meeting or event she needs to go to. He comes to the Kishore Kumar building and starts an onward journey to its second floor. The cool entrance hits his face and body. As he stands near the elevator the golden frames of Kishore Kumar, Mohammed Rafi, Lata Mangeshkar, Manna Dey, and Hemant Mukhopadhyay loom large. When he was a child Baba used to listen to patriotic and devotional songs by these stalwarts on his transistor radio. That's how he fell in love with the voice of Kishore Kumar. Quietly Kabir picked each of his songs and sang them in his style, made them his own until tunes of his making began visiting him. He dreamt of one day like Kishore Kumar making the whole world sit up and listen to him.

The elevator brings Kabir to the second floor. He sees the array of studio doors. Girls in strangely loose, colourful attire and fashionable glasses run around with large paper cups of Starbucks coffee in their hands. They look like assistants serving some big playback singer or actors who must be dubbing their parts in this building which is mainly dedicated to sound work. He spots the studio number he's supposed to enter. As he gently opens the door and enters a loud sound of chorus singing reaches his ears. The words are despicable. This can't be his room; he quickly steps back and looks for someone to ask for guidance. One of the assistant girls looks at the address on Kabir's phone. She directs him to the same door he just walked out of. It raises a doubt in him, is this where Anu wanted him to come?

Kabir enters the studio this time. It's a larger hall where in one section four to five men are singing the same chorus. A tall, thin man with his long hair tied back is directing them. Kabir waits for them to stop so he can ask whom he's supposed to meet. Kabir is too shy to ask too many questions. A constant fear guides him as if asking an extra question will lead to someone marking him for not being capable somewhere. He hesitantly asks the man, "Manish ji? Is that you?" the man turns back restless. He looks at Kabir and gets it, he signals him towards the group of chorus singers who right now like lost cattle are waiting to be told by Manish how bad they are. Kabir is completely confused by now. He tries to show the address and details that Anu has sent on his phone. He mutters, "Sir, I am here for Play Back, Lead?" The desire to sing is now bursting through Kabir's skin more than ever before.

Manish breaks out into a peal of ugly laughter. He takes Kabir by his jacket and pulls him to a distant glass box. A recording is going on. The lead playback singer of the time Ankush Singh is singing away. He is lost in his singing with a band of assistants, and production people waiting for him in the same section of the hall where the chorus singers are rehearsing. Manish points at them, "You see them? They are his Paltan, they wipe his ass and feed him and take him from place to place. Do you know why? Cause he makes that kind of money!! Now either sing this chorus or get lost." Manish's voice thunders in the large hall while the star continues to sing oblivious of the drama unfolding outside his glass box. His entourage, the chorus singers are still, watching Manish shout at Kabir. Kabir feels his skin burning, the lump in his throat almost about to make him burst into tears. This is worse than the impact of Vineet, it is happening inside the very place he considers to be a pilgrimage centre. The Star Studio.

But he cannot cry, he must pull it off like a case of mistaken identity. After Manish is done speaking Kabir gently raises his head and says, "Sorry I came into the wrong studio. I am the Lead Singer in another Production." Without waiting for a second Kabir turns to leave, feeling the stupefied eyes of the occupants of the hall digging into his back. Manish calls out, "Any more samples outside? Please send. Strange are the expectations of these bastards". Though the door opened briefly to shut behind Kabir immediately he heard the acid remark.

He comes down to flush out of the premises of Star Studio. The marble temple continues with the loud chants of "Shri Krishna Govind Hare Muraari" indifferent to the raw pain and stab in his chest. An aged Pandit is doing an Aarti, the staff are gathered and technicians from various floors pray. Though each is lost in his or her oblivion of the mythical success-finding journey, Kabir almost feels a thousand eyes boring into his skin. As he comes near the bike, his being, his organ he looks at it and hates the very object which he loved so dearly. It feels like a lifeless, metal cage he had chosen to keep himself trapped in. He gives it one last look and walks away towards the main gate. At the main gate, the guards see him walk out. One of them calls out for his token but Kabir will not look back. Not anymore, he knows where he needs to go and whom to confront.

Though rickshaws abound outside Star Studio, Kabir chooses to walk past the queue of hopefuls, he takes a closer look at the man with the placard. The road is dusty and narrowed down with no space to walk by as digging of the roads abounds in every corner and crevice of this part of the city. It's a gas supply line this time.

It is a long way and yet he walks with the sounds of car horns and honking blaring at him, sometimes he almost gets into the trajectory of a car. Suddenly a large, plush car comes to a jolting halt as Kabir crosses his path looking down. He suddenly realizes he is standing still in the middle of the road. A passerby races to take Kabir away from the trajectory of the car. As Kabir is led away, he sees the person at the steering wheel. Despite the pain and humiliation raging in his heart Kabir knows, it's her, its Smouldering Eyes. And she's seen him too. It seems like she where almost about to get out of the car and call out for him. He gives a smirk saying under his breath 'Miss Cinderella', he then quickly melts into the thick crowd racing towards Andheri station thus rubbing off his existence into anonymity.

After about an hour of walking and feeling thirsty and hungry and a thick vale of dust in the air clogging his face and hair Kabir reaches Anu's abode. It's too early to ring her bell, Kabir knows her nuances, and timings in detail. He's never gone out of the way with her, has been like a dog with his faithfulness and kindness and bearing it all. He rings the bell again and again, today he will wait for no etiquette shit. The nerves in his forehead are throbbing with acidic anger. Finally, Anu opens the door, she hates waking early as she must have finished a late-night event to come back only at Three in the morning. She greets Kabir lovingly, knowing he must be coming directly from the studio. She extends her hand to reach out for him. He grunts, "I need to come in and say a few things after which I will leave."

Anu is not able to gauge what's going on with Kabir since contrary to being overwhelmed by the opportunity provided to him, Kabir is agitated. She moves aside for him to step in. He pulls out the bike key and places it in her hand. "Here, the vehicle is still at the Star Studio complex, ask someone to get it picked up, my need for it has ended. Thank you for everything you have done for me so far." Anu stares at the keys, she has a sharp sense of things coming to an end between her and Kabir. This is not why she invested her money and attention on him all these years, she wants to keep him as her's. She mutters, "Kabir, your recording didn't go well? I even checked with Darshan last night! He had said he would guide you" Kabir now finds this unbearable, and flares up, "Guide me? All you sent me to sing is the chorus in some horrendous soundtrack! And now you pretend you don't know a thing? You thought it would be gratifying enough for me to just step into Star Studio? Or feel so scared of the entire experience that I wouldn't want to go into the uncertainty of a hit or flop and would rather choose to run back and be your lap dog? I don't need this." As Kabir yells, the old obese cook Celine comes out of the kitchen. She has been, over the years, working away in Anu's kitchen to keep Anu's keto meals, apples, avocados, and sugar-free desserts of the other managers and models, and Kabir's non-apologetic spicy, fish curry and rice all in place.

Celine looks on at Kabir who has always been a sweet, submissive boy. He turns to leave and Anu walks after him.

"Kabir you are angry, come back when you feel better, let me check with Darshan what happened?" Kabir turns to reply sharply, "No, I don't want you to look into anything Anu, we are done." Anu calls out angered now, "you ungrateful bastard, call people to do your publicity, plead people to hear you once, train you, groom you, and then you piss on me and go. Don't ever come back then, don't ever call me." The last few words of Anu have reached Kabir. He is today reminded again and again of his Baba. Today he wants to reach out to those large arms of the tall, large-built Pobon whom the entire village called Pobon Khyepa (crazed one).

But no one notices Anu's moistened eyes that fill with the memory and lost hope, the same vapid emptiness of her partner again. She walks to the Bar, Celine tries and soothes her with a gentle pat on her back. Anu shirks off her hand asking for a salad to go with her drink. She recklessly looks into her phone looking for something to keep her busy.

Kabir takes an auto and goes close to home, somewhere in the back lanes of Andheri West where he's earlier knocked on the doors of the Bars and Lounges to allow him to sing on the weekends. He remembers how much money he has stashed away at home in a cardboard box and how many rupees are in his savings bank account. Anu will block the card, stop the payment of his rent, and probably also get him thrown out of the building complaining to the housing committee about him.

Till late evening Kabir sits in Blue Door Lounge at a corner table and drinks until he is heavy, drowsy, and unable to think. He gets up and asks for the bill. As he takes out the currency notes from his back pocket, the thick visiting card the enterprising Siridevi had left with him emerges. He looks at the odd diamond mark in the center of it. And sees the number beneath it. As they clear the bill Kabir runs his fingers on the thick card, a part of him is wailing for help. A part says to pack up and leave, this is the end. He has to call his broker, ask for the notice period, gather everything, empty his flat, and leave the city. He has to go back to Dhulishor, lie low for a year, and then think of his life ahead. For the first time, Kabir considers submitting to his Baba as the only way out, and hates himself bitterly for even thinking about it.

Kabir flushes out into the darkness. The lanes are only beginning to fill up with the evening crowd. Kabir begins to walk though his legs are shaky. He enters a lane which is a shortcut from the by-lanes into the main road. He has some money, he will go to Juhu beach and watch the waves till late at night. Kabir can't bear the thought of going home and in this state. Tanvi Chaachi will ask a thousand questions and the children will tease him calling him a 'beowra' (drunkard).

As Kabir softly walks into the lane he hears a whisper in the air. He knows the smell of fresh weed, he's smelt it at the parties at Anu's sometimes. Her supplier Jolly used to bring in pouches and he was the first one she used to share it with. Then throughout the night, it would be a wild party of devouring each other. As Kabir feels an unknown fear like an animal about to be attacked, he considers turning and going back but this is when he feels a sharp jolt in his arm. It's a sharp cut and he is profusely bleeding.

He can now see the shadow of two or three boys, the weed smelling stronger than ever before. They look into his shirt and

, search his pockets. One of them gets to feel the thin gold chain with an Om hanging around his neck. This was not one of Anu's gifts. His Baba had given it to him on his ninth birthday, melting away all his mother's jewels which he didn't want to keep, to make the memories more painful. She died when Kabir was three, a constant mate and partner, Kabir's mother Suhasini had left Pobon with the purpose of bringing up this child in the world as their only sign of having been together. The boys have got to the chain and are sure they will snatch it from Kabir. He requests, "Please not this one, it's my only…" without waiting for a second one of them snatches it hard enough to tear away from Kabir's neck leaving a sharp cut from which a trail of blood streams down his neck. They race away into the lights of the nighttime city. Kabir flops on the dust of the anonymous, deserted lane and buries his head between his knees in despair and hopelessness. He yells but his sound is muted in the scheme of things, he has nothing and that's a fine place to be in, in this city. An occasional passerby walks past cautiously. The slash in his arm is bleeding as is the snap at his neck, but Kabir gets on his trembling feet. He wipes his face with his arm, pulling himself up with great difficulty he comes up to the main road and gets into an auto. Once in the auto, he gasps while the driver is busy on his earphones connected to his home in Bihar. Kabir calls out, "Aram Nagar".

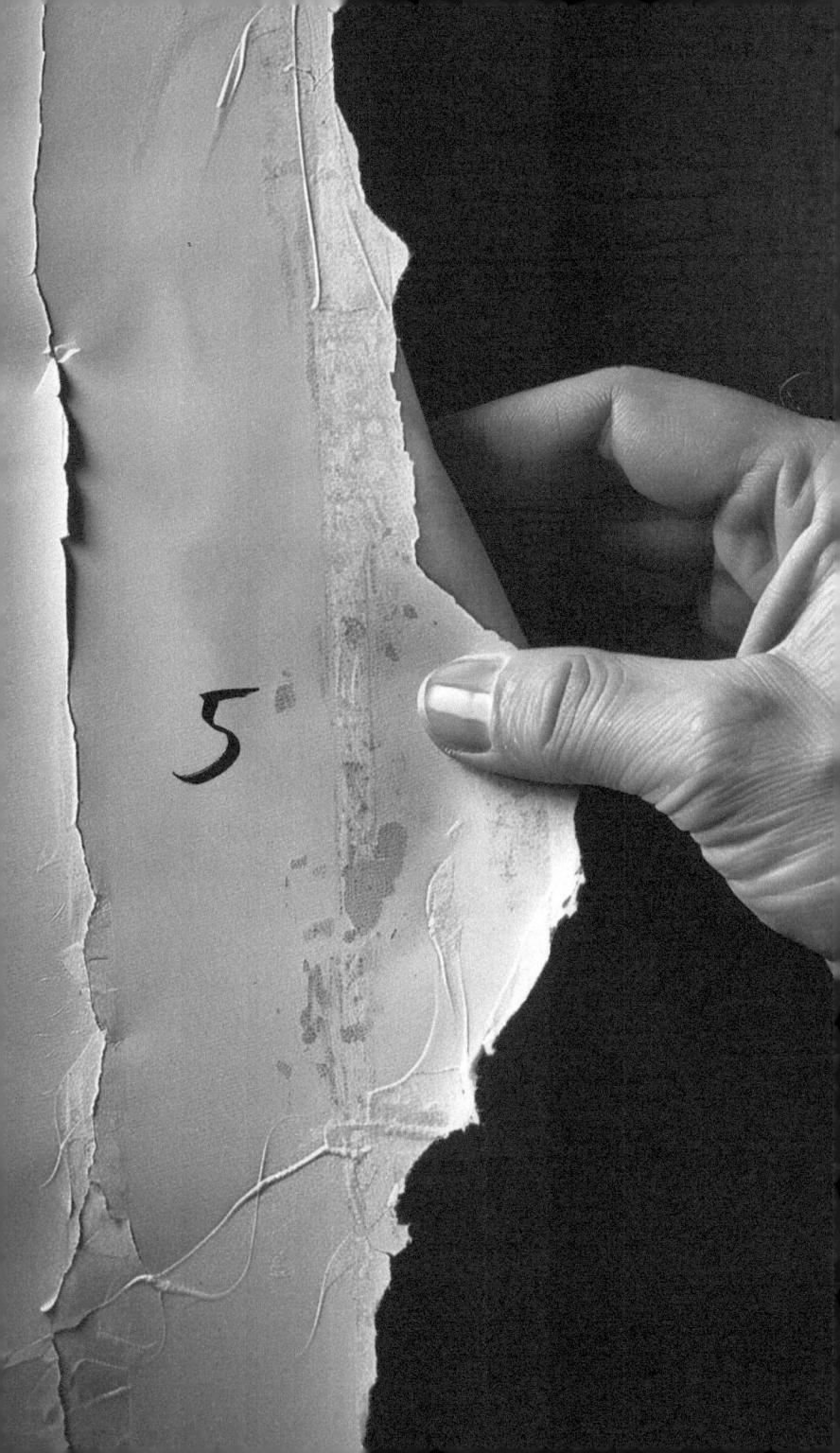

Green, blue, yellow, and purple lights blaze as the soundtrack of "Choli ke peeche kya hai.." comes alive on the dance floor of Siridevi's bungalow. Somewhere in the pits of broken, crammed Aaram Nagar. Siridevi takes centre stage letting the gay boys spread around her. She removes her shawl, she is in a dazzling ghagra choli, a flimsy dupatta caressing her pushed-up breasts, her hair shining in gold under the lights. Tall, thick, and dark Don stands near the door with his large, muscular body keeping an eagle-like, lusty gaze on Siridevi.

As the seductive song begins Siridevi stands in the centre and rhythm with the boys begins to gyrate her masculine hips while throwing up her breasts provocatively. The slender, gay boys follow her rhythm, trying to match her energy and speed. As they gently twist and turn their hips Siridevi eyeing them through her dupatta suddenly comes raging, hits one of them on his hips with her thick hand. "Not like that you chutiyaa, bundle of nerves, let it go, look at me again." With this, she again goes back to the centre and in the floating neon lights lets her light and brisk body float like a gentle and lithe swan with a raw ball of energy in its centre which none can predict will go which way. Just then a loud thump is heard on the paper-thin door. Once, then twice. Don looks at Siridevi questioningly. Siridevi knows that thump, that urgency, she signals him to open the door while signaling one of the gay boys to turn off the music.

A tired, panting Kabir stands at the door. His arm and neck, still bleeding. The sight of him makes Siridevi breathless, or so it seems. She lets the dupatta fall, she races to Kabir, and brings him gently to the springy sofa that has been serving the purpose of letting the students keep their bags and props. She shouts out at them, "Remove all this shit load junk you bitch, get me the first aid box." For the next half an hour Siridevi gently nurses Kabir and bandages his raw and deep knife wound. One of them rushes to a close by coffee joint to bring him a cold sandwich.

Kabir hungrily bites into it while Siridevi gently runs her hand on his ruffled, matted head. Time ticks away, tears roll down Kabir's eyes. Tears of pain, humiliation. Siridevi gently picks up his trembling hand and kisses it. "Such a talented singer and yet, look at his state, why my Jaanu? Mera Raaja!! Who did this to you? Tell me. We have our ways to get even." Kabir shirks away her response and slowly gets up to occupy the centre of the hall. He looks into the eyes of Siridevi to say what he needs to, "I thought I would leave this city; I thought I would go back. But not until the last door is shut on me, not yet. Give me work, any song any tune... anything. I will do it like no one else can." His words reach Siridevi and begin to impact her. A jealous Don keeps his gaze fixed on Kabir with animosity. Something inside Siridevi is filling up with deep contentment, she opens her arms wide for a hug. She knows the iron is hot, that the strike must happen now, for the metal to acquire its desired shape, her desired shape.

As Kabir's vision blurs in pain, he can feel movement happen in the room. Someone goes and brings back something to Siridevi, that is the large, muscular Don. They exchange a look of understanding. As Siridevi takes it lovingly from his hand and brings it close to Kabir, he realizes it is a bundle of papers and a leaking ballpoint pen. Kabir in the blur signs the papers. There is nothing more to think about in matters of trust, nowhere else to look. For a frail second his Baba's face visits him. But he lets that pass by and signs the document in all places, in a scribble. As soon as he has signed Siridevi signals Don to offer sweets to Kabir and everyone. While Don obediently brings a paper box of Pedas which is magically ready and waiting, Kabir turns it away politely, he is anxious, and hungry with only one question. "What next? Where are you taking me?" Siridevi gently runs her long cold hand on Kabir's face, letting the edges of her pink nails sharply make an effect on him. "Soon, soon we will make you sing, you go home, sleep and tomorrow we will meet you in Star Studio, the same recording room that you left humiliated this morning".

Kabir for the first time feels the need to be comfortable, stop worrying, calculating. Everything in this large city can't be a what's-the-big-catch game. Perhaps there are places in the world where one can look for help, hold a hand, and rise again. By now it's anyhow too late to think, he has to survive this abyss and at that, this is the best he can do. The music gets louder, and the smell of a rare and pungent hash is very strong in the air. The lights swim, Don brings a cigarette close to Kabir, and he smokes without resistance. A deep, deep, breath, a pull followed by more pulls. The head loosens, it's like years of load taken off his back and head. How did he just get here? How could it be so easy and all in a day or two? Was it this close? Kabir smokes away harder, and the music thrives. He tells himself, "Yes, sometimes things are that close".

Kabir wakes up to a touch. Siridevi is looking down at him as he is lying on the sofa in the same hall where he was last night. She is gently touching him on his forehead, she is in a mask covering her dark skin. As Kabir gets up, he is taken aback by the transgender's actual face which must have sharp bristles on her cheeks and chin, her skin is glistening now devoid of the peach pancake she pats on all day. The makeup around her eyes is still not fully erased. "Here, all this is for you my Jaanu, your day begins now." She holds out a large packet and a Starbucks cup of steaming coffee. Kabir takes the packet, it is full of branded clothes, and slippers. He smiles at them.

Sofi enters Star Studio a little nervous. She's late. She exactly knows where Hamid is. Hamid has been here for years. He restores old works. That's his job, quietly, patiently he restores forgotten voices, and memories. Sofi balances a large stack of cassettes and places them on his table. Hamid is too preoccupied with his work work; the studio always has old soundtracks to restore. He looks at them, Sofi urges him, "I have come with a lot of hope Chaacha. Please help me." Hamid is not too easily interested in working with the young. "Whose are they?" he asks, looking up from what he is doing ready to dismiss her. "Sangeeta Mishra ji," says Sofi hoping to grab his attention. He now comes up from the console gently and lends them a look as if in the lifeless stack of audio cassettes, he can suddenly see a face, a person. He looks up at Sofi as she removes her goggles. A little blue bump floats under her right eye though she's concealed it well. "My mother Chacha, now I have to get them converted." Hamid now looks at Sofi with a renewed gaze, "You are Sangeeta ji's daughter?" Sofi nods knowing Hamid has been an ardent admirer of his mother. Her eyes moisten at the thought of her mother. Every time she mentions her name, her voice, that evening surfaces, an evening of her last time with her mother. And then comes the question that the whole world keeps asking her, "Whatever happened to Sangeeta Mishra ji?" Sofi stares at Hamid blankly.

She has no answers, she hopes her silence conveys enough. He bows his head for a moment of silence, paying his respect to her. "Very few knew her kind of music, her kind of rendition. You, beta ji, never wanted to sing?" Sofi now quickly takes charge as she must. She covers up her brief moments of grief, "No Chaacha, I have everything the world could ask me to have. My only mission is to save these tapes of my mother, her voice at day's end is my anchor. For years I have had them recorded on my phone but now the originals will die. While the world chooses to know her by only one song these are all composed and sung by her." Hamid holds the tapes differently.

He then turns on a knob in the console, only to hear a loud and brash voice sing, "Meow Meow" It is shrill, and it throws off Sofi. She blocks her ears, and Hamid bursts out into laughter. "That's the sound of today my beta ji!" while Hamid says so Sofi deeply focuses on the voice. She knows how to connect with voices, she doesn't forget them. She calls out, "I know this voice Chaacha, but this song? For how long will this go on? Where is this recording happening?" Hamid gets up and shows Sofi the recording room. He gives her a slip with a date to come back for her mother's cassettes. She nods and walks away but her feet take her towards the 'Meow Meow' recording hall instead of the main door. As Sofi gently opens the thick, heavy door and walks into the large studio she chooses a dark corner for herself. The recording has just come to an end. The chimpanzee barks so long from the glass box in strange baggy clothes that blare brands, and a heavy-set dark eyeglass flushes out of the glass box. They are thrilled, they hug, and an entourage begins to take photographs. Sofi is not more disturbed than ever before, of course, she knows this voice but this clown she fails to identify. As the flashes keep going Sofi finally realizes who he is. This is the man with the voice in the Marriott coffee shop, the man whose number she hunted down and met on the beach to hear him sing, the very man who would have met with an accident near Star Studio almost walking into her car. The man with a distinct voice, a voice as deep as the shade of a banyan tree. As turbulent as an oceanic roar. The first voice, the first evening, the first taste of the man never left her.

The clock steadily trots, Sofi stares at Kabir grabbing it all and more. Then Siridevi stops them all, she kisses Kabir and tells him to go, he needs to now rest his voice. Kabir wishes them all one last goodbye and flushes out while Siridevi attends to the media glare and answers their questions patiently. Sofi quietly follows Kabir as he moves out of the studio to walk in the direction of the elevators. He is still whistling the 'Meow Meow' tune. As he impatiently waits for the lift Sofi touches him on his shoulder. He turns around, a tiny skip in her heart. Though he is a little high and excited with a false charm his eyes know her, Smouldering Eyes of course. She's caused him enough trouble already. Why is she here? Has she been following him? She calls out, "Hey you, singer of Chal kahi.."

Kabir hates the mention of this, he doesn't want to go there, he doesn't need to. He looks around to see if anyone is hearing or has followed him from the studio. He softly replies with equal sarcasm, "Yes Miss Cinderella? Here you come! What do you want now? One moment you appear the next you disappear, haven't you had enough of my service?? Now please get out of my way." The lift is climbing towards him, and Kabir is waiting to jump into it, her eyes are like a pair of magnets, they won't let him look elsewhere. Sofi continues, "That you, were a far better you! That singing, your voice was thunder! What do you think you are doing to yourself in the name of music here?" The lift has arrived. As it opens wide and Kabir flushes in before the doors can slide back, he gives Sofi a look, "Naam, paisa, rutbaa, sab chahiye mujhe. Chaapna hai..buss ab chaapna hai. (I need name, money, and fame, I need it all. And mint money like it's no one's business!) So, you can keep your lectures on art, music, and creativity for some article you want to publish and, in the process, also expect fame. We all want the same things so don't fucking stop me". With this the doors close, and the lift glides down. Sofi stares at the closed doors of the lift, her heart still beating, responding to this man. She is muddled in her head, whether to go back to Hamid to give him a few instructions or to rush down with the next lift and look for Kabir. There is no explanation for why she wants to go look for him but a part of her wants to. But as she stops herself to check her watch, she knows her Cinderella hour is coming to an end.

The outside is hot, robustly loud, and bustling. Kabir gets into the sprawling, yellow Audi that has been taking him from one place to the other now. The driver knows where to drop him, but Kabir gets busy with his phone. They have launched 'Meow Meow' in the studio itself, Siridevi had promised that by the time he will be in his car it will already be out there, in the public domain. He feeds his ID into the social media accounts and awaits. There it is, 'Meow Meow', his voice blares through the roof while the likes, hits of hearts, and thumbs up at the bottom of the screen rise. He can't believe it, he's seen this happen to others, and he's known it to be a way of establishing the song as a hit. As the Audi comes to a halt at the tedious Juhu Circle signal Kabir's eyes meet a strange sight. A group of Bauls are being led across the street. They are probably going to a function close by. Their long-matted hair, their patchwork Alkhalaas, and the Dotaaras they cradle in their arms, stir memories afresh. He stares at the screen of his phone and then goes to the contacts list. He stares at the word- Baba. Then gathering a little strength, he dials the number. One ring, two rings, no voice at the other end. No one picks up, and the call cuts. The signals turn green, the car flushes into his section of the city, and a tear trickles down Kabir's eye.

As he comes to the crooked broken lane outside his almost-invisible building he calls out to the driver a little embarrassed, "its ok Ji, you can drop me here and leave." he can see from the corner of his eyes a flamboyant Tanvi holding Alien close sitting near the stairs at the entrance, the children playing are looking at the car curiously, in seconds they will be here. But the driver has other instructions. He smiles back warmly, "No problem, Sir, it is my duty to stay with you." He sits still with not an extra word after that. Kabir steps out of the car knowing the children will come rushing. They come by him as they look unusually cautious. One of them signals at the car and asks if that's his, he winks and nods. A whistle, a cheer, they are thrilled. "Bhaiyaa Meow Meow..hit your song is a hit." They show a cheap phone one of them brings out of his pocket, his voice is audible in the very place he wanted it to be heard. Tanvi eyes him but doesn't make the effort to come up. She must have heard about his song from the children, she knows it's doing the rounds in the right places, but she is not happy. Kabir gives her a flying kiss and walks by letting her be.

Once he is home in the silence and cool darkness, he stares at the large photograph of Pobon. His heart is overflowing with love and tears for him. The man who taught him the tunes and the rhythms, the man without whose support he couldn't have been. Kabir takes out his phone and dials Pobon's number again. The phone is engaged at first, then the second time it rings, and Pobon picks up. There's a loud chant going on in the background. There's a still quality to everything. He knows this mantra. Pobon used to perform puja, and rites in homes for income in the months when monsoon or the cold would prevent him from singing in places far from home. This is the Shraadh mantra (last rites), someone has died, something come to an end. "Baba? Who?" Kabir asks and awaits an answer. After a long pause the aged Baul calls out, "You, you died for me. For all of us here in Dhulishor." It takes the breath out of Kabir. Why would his Baba say this? On a day when people are finally hearing his voice in the open, the day he has been waiting for so long. Kabir's voice wavers, "Baba, my song is out.." but before he can say another word his Baba stops him. "I heard it Kabir, and only after that did, I kill you inside of me. Until now I had some faint hope, that Ishwar will give you sense, and drive you to do something correctly. And maybe in that dry, arid land, He will give you a tune. But if this is what you have birthed, if this is who you are then I truly don't want you. No one in the village believes it could be you." A loud beep is heard on Kabir's vapid face. As if something had been sucked out of him, his gut drops. In a deep fear of his father's conscience having left him, Kabir drowns in a strange half-sleep half-awake state. Sometimes Pobon sometimes Smouldering Eyes continue to visit him.

The phone purring on his wooden bed stand wakes up Kabir. It's Siridevi singing softly to him, "Uth meri jaan!! Tera bulaawa aa hi gayaa hai, finally!!" (wake up dearest, your turn has come). Kabir is curious, and wonders if it's another song she wants him to come and record. He remains silent, Siridevi continues cooing, "The car will come to you in an hour, get ready and dashing, today the mistress has requested for you!" Mistress reminds Kabir of Anu. He is repulsed by the idea of another older woman holding him by his need. "Siridevi ..listen , please listen I am very thankful for the song but I don't want to again become a toy boy of some rich woman, that's not me anymore. Anywhere else you can send me." Siridevi smiles gently but speaks viciously. "But our mistress is a kind soul, it is she who saw your defeat and brought you your first song while your Anu..." The rest need not be told. "Welcome to the club my Jaanu, this is all you must have been waiting for all these years. Now you will be seen differently, perceived differently, you are one of them, the successful people." Kabir begins to feel a lightness in his being as Siridevi's words pour into his ears.

Kabir gets up as the day is coming to an end, and takes a hot bath, letting his pores wake up, his scalp feeling the hot water. And then in a shirt and denim, a light jacket he steps out knowing the yellow Audi will be waiting for him at the rusted, broken gate of Kadam Chawl. He waves at the children at a distance, at Tanvi and Alien. While looking disinterested in him, Kabir knows she is stuck at the main gate keeping a close track of where he goes, and who comes to pick him up. She can smell fame. As Kabir waves at her she waves back coldly. Often those who claim to love us do so as they find us in the same place as theirs. The love is tested only when one of our positions is changed. Kabir has shot up; the rest have gone down under. This is the new equation, now they don't like him anymore.

Once inside the plush car, he checks the rows of tiny alcohol bottles neatly placed in a case between the back seats, the music is a strange trance. The car races through the highway, and he is unable to gauge which way it is taking him. He stares at his phone; the network seems to have oddly gone. They leave the highway and enter a narrow pathway. But somewhere close to the sea. Kabir calls out over the trance, "Madh?" the driver nods gently. After another hour of driving into the interiors, they reach the precincts of a large, spread-out villa. Kabir flushes out of the car and the moment he steps out the yellow Audi swooshes past him. He is left staring at the villa calling out to him. After a few seconds as if on cue the iron gates open making way for Kabir. Something tells him he is entering another space and checks his phone; it is still out of network.

As Kabir enters the gates a large lawn welcomes him. A garage at a distance, stares back at him with a fleet of about five cars standing in a row. He comes near them to remove the thick hood of each and take a peep. Cars draw him, their make fascinates him. They are of all sorts. Porsche, Rolls Royce, Mustang, a fiercely red Ferrari with number 1 shrieking out of its number plate. Just when he is about to check the fifth one, he hears a sound. Of something moving, a sharp sound of hitting an object. He moves in its direction and what stares back at him is a large glistening swimming pool. Standing near its edge is a stout midget in a maroon coat, trousers and hat all made out of the same cloth material. He is using a tong-like instrument to kill a snake violently while adjusting a net like an expert in another hand in which the reptile is struggling. After a few more plunges the reptile seems to have died while its tail end peeping out of the net is still moving. Even before Kabir can call out, he takes the net to the side of the pool and dashes the dead reptile with a thick boulder kept beside it. Kabir watches this site repulsed, wondering what this world is, and who are the people who live here. And who is this mistress of his music he's come to meet? While the midget now throws away the body of the snake into a pile and sets it on fire Kabir calls out, "Suniye?" (Hey you over there!) The midget turns to Kabir and knowing he is expected bends down to wash his hands in the pool and then patting his moist hands against his thick coat rushes in his direction. As he nears Kabir, Kabir notices his face is painted chalk white with his eyes and mouth circled in red. "Arrey Meow Meow Saab, aaiye aaiye! Sorry, garmi mein saanp bohot pareshaan kartey hai."(Oh Sir, it's you the singer of Meow Meow! The snakes trouble a lot in the summer) Having said this the midget produces his stubby hand, "Me Rancho! You Mr Kabir?" Kabir shakes hands knowing a few minutes ago he was touching, battering the reptile with that same hand.

The tall door of the villa opens, and Rancho shows Kabir the way into its cold interior. The lights are dim, and the furniture is leisurely put together but not out of place. Someone has carefully chosen the curtains, furnishing, and artefacts in almost every corner. A well-replenished Bar shines in a corner. Rancho signals Kabir to sit while with an athletic leap, he jumps onto one of the Bar stools and goes to the other side. He calls out from the other side, "Saab very good whiskey we have, please have, then I go and tell Madam." Kabir is in his hands; he nods without much choice. Within the next two to three minutes Rancho disappears behind the Bar to fix Kabir's drink. Kabir looks around, behind the thick curtains the deserted lawn and pool stare back. He is forced to ask, "Party kahaa hai?" (where the hell is the party?). He is beginning to feel a little scared and yet he knows this is supposed to be a place of trust for him. "Basement Sir" calls out Rancho while making the drink and passing in three heart-shaped pink pills into the thick drink. They dissolve in seconds, Rancho smiles through his yellowed teeth. Perhaps the mistress lives a remote life and hopes to hear him here, with her close circuit of friends. This could be the beginning of his first meaningful professional relationship with a company, after all a company is a person on the top. Rancho has arrived with the stiff whiskey. He smiles exposing his yellowed teeth standing out in his white face. "Here Sir!" As Kabir takes the glass Rancho bows gently and walks back. Before he can pass out through a large door on the other side he calls out, "Drink Sir, I tell her you are here."

Night has fallen as is visible through the large curtains allowing a little view of the outside. Kabir sips into the drink, the whiskey rolling down into his gut bringing something alive in him. He feels more awake on a deeper level than ever before about a fact. Someone somewhere is watching, looking at him on a screen, a camera hanging right above his head concealed in confetti on the wall. Kabir thirstily drinks away the full glass, as he keeps it aside. The pink heart tablets have left their last particles at the bottom of the glass while the rest is racing in Kabir's bloodstream. His head is feeling lighter, much lighter, and a strange bounce persists in his being. It is only when he decides to get up and look around the room that Kabir realizes his feet feel wobbly as if his blood has turned into the spirit and his flesh into balls of cotton. His vision feels slightly blurred when he notices the large door on the other side open and Rancho peers at him. He signals Kabir to follow, Kabir rests his feet one after the other on the floor carefully like it were a humongous task and walks up to Rancho. He can almost fly, His head and body by now are so light.

They walk down a strange corridor. Kabir looks on either side. The walls are adorned with stuffed heads of deer, boars, and large antlers. Skull portraits persist, metallic skulls, leathery skulls, furry skulls. In thick frames and then they arrive at a glass staircase that leads them downwards. Rancho picks a thick candle stand kept at the edge of the staircase. He lights it and shows Kabir the way into the semi-lit basement. By now Kabir has lost his sense of questioning, a floating feeling persists allowing him to be taken wherever. And a perfume invades him, calling him to itself.

Climbing down about ten or twelve steps they land on a floor of white walls, white ceilings, white corridors, and red lights flashing all over. That smell that Kabir was hit by earlier now gets stronger. Rancho shows the way into what seems like a large hall with wooden flooring. The entire hall is filled with candles. And in its centre swims a tall, thick, golden bed. Somewhere near the bed is a booth covered with flimsy, red curtains. And around the bed are bodies skimpily dressed, their eyes covered in masks that grow into horns. Rancho looks at Kabir knowing he is deeply aroused even without his need to be so. On the bed lies a figure not yet fully clear to Kabir but he finds it impossible to hold himself back as Rancho walks him closer to the bed. Horn Head watches closely.

One of the figures bends down to whisper into the ear of the figure lying down. As the news passes on, they all break into a strange dance holding hands, and they begin to circle the bed. A trance music rolls out and even before Kabir can ask or say a thing Rancho holds him by his hand and with all might throws Kabir into the tall bed. The woman is concealed inside a thick quilt, her face concealed by a metallic mask. The girls continue to circle them and sing a low tune. Metallic Mask pulls him into the thick, warm blanket after which Kabir loses touch with his own body. Amidst flashes of wildly letting the woman dig herself into his aroused body, Kabir sees Horn Head in the booth. Is he masturbating? Kabir takes quick breaths, finding it tough to cope with the pushes, the thrusts, the pulls. At a point in time, he feels the circling girls closer to them, he can feel more hands touching him, the light lull is now a chant, and louder and louder they sing. Horn Head is standing, bending over watching each action on the bed, he is almost about to ejaculate. Kabir loses his senses and passes out in the arms of Metallic Mask.

The yellow rays of morning light hit Kabir's eyes. He squints, squeezes, then opens them to find out where he is. Whose bed was he in and where is he now? Kabir feels the cold first and realizes his torso is bare. It's laden with dust and twigs and so is his face and hair. He looks around him as his vision clears out. He is in the middle of the forest surrounding the Madh Island Highway. From a distance, he can hear vehicles coming and going but he can't find the strength to get up. His denims feel soggy, the earth is wet with morning dew and damp collected on it. With great difficulty despite a blaring headache, Kabir pulls himself up. Something strikes and he checks in his pocket. His phone is still there with him and as if like magic it is back to network. The battery is fading, but he manages to call for an Uber setting in it his current location which he now notices is the highway.

Kabir gently trudges on his shivering feet and comes up to the highway, drivers, and helpers in passing vehicles stare at him. As he anxiously awaits getting into a vehicle to somehow go back to the city, Kabir tries to remember the night gone by. Flashes of the drink that the midget gave him, the perfume in the underbelly of the villa, figures dancing, and the forceful thrusts of a woman with her masked face come to him. The dark sockets of her eyes, the breath breezing in from the holes in her nose reach him even now. The Uber drives up to him. As he gets into the car, he tells the code to the driver and passes out on the seat. The journey seems never-ending. But Kabir doesn't stop at Kadam Chawl, he gets off at Aram Nagar.

In the pits of the Madh villa the nights are endless, the days hidden and long. Metal Mask is wide awake, lazing, calling for a stiff black coffee. Lying beside her is her Horn Head who must have slithered into her bed in the early hours of dawn. Sensing she is awake Horn Head stirs and tries pulling her to himself. Metal Mask lets him touch her; he tries to engage with her in a kiss. Not a nerve in her body makes a stirring. But one look at Horn Head and she is repulsed. She pushes him away and reaches out for her phone. She shows him the photo she took last night. Of the boy who came to them last night. The same boy, the same fiery face, inward-looking eyes, that boy with a voice whose video Vimla had sent from the Marriott coffee shop, now she only wants him. She like a vampire sucked on his raw energy and finds her desire returning to her with vengeance. They must have picked him from his bed to throw him in a place of anonymity for no recall of the night he passed. But the aches and pulls in his muscles will tell him he was here, he was here in the bed, the death trap of the Black Widow. She calls Siridevi, guzzles, "Usse bulaa, use phir bulaa. Gaadi de de, bunglaa de de, wo chahiye mujhe" (call for him again, give him a car, a house whatever he might need, he has to be here for me.) Horn Head is taken aback by her demand, he holds her hands with his large muscular hands and pins them down to devour her breasts. She calls out for her chambermaids. Siridevi cuts the call, and smiles on her own. She returns to the foreigners she is attending to in the Aram Nagar bungalow.

The bungalow seems busy with activity. Kabir races in to find her at her tiny chamber talking to three or four foreigners. Impressing them with her broken English while Don stands guard behind her. Upon seeing Kabir, Don steps forward. Something instinctively tells him that Kabir will attack Siridevi. Siridevi signals Don to take Kabir aside. Kabir, without making things tough steps into the next room. Don pushes a towel and throws at him a jacket and a mineral water bottle. Kabir calls out, "Jaldi, nahi toh sab kuch tod dunga yahaa" (make that fast or else I will break everything). As Don stands guard making sure Kabir won't leap into the next room ten minutes pass by. Words float in, Siridevi is making a deal. They are Russians offering shoot at high subsidy in St Petersburg. And Siridevi keeps referring to someone as Our Star, "Our star will come, our star has many songs..our star is a real super duper star!!" After they have been convinced that the so-called star is a great buy they walk away and Siridevi in her stilettoes walks them out.

She then comes into Kabir's section. Her sweetness and overt concern hits Kabir. She comes and hugs him like she where only waiting for him. Even before he can say a word, she drowns him in kisses on his cheeks, on his forehead, and takes the Pallu of her thick, zardozi saree to bless him. Kabir shrugs off with a "huh...kahaa bheji thi mujhe?" (Where the hell did you send me?) Siridevi now sits back and lets Don serve her a green tea. She sips and says, "To my Maalkin? Maai Baap oh how she loved you, my Jaanu. She loved being with you so much, she can't wait for you again." While Siridevi looks ecstatic Kabir stares at her disgusted, in disbelief. "You think I am going back to that hell hole? That pit where you sent me? And this is how they leave me? Throw me away in the forest? This is over now, once and for all." Kabir is about to get up and leave.

Siridevi gets up to stop him on his way out. She gently touches Kabir and allows her long finger to run over his nose. He turns away, but she persists. "Eh Jaanu, why are you angry?

So much work I am doing for you, don't you see? Now we will go to Russia to shoot your next song. Three songs Madam has sent already for you to record. Hit hit hit songs!! Hai naa?" Having said it all Siridevi looks at Kabir closely. It makes sense to him. At whatever level they operate they are making a way, a chance for him to work it out. At least he is a known voice now out there in the void. He softens a bit. "When will you give me the next recording?" Now Siridevi begins to push Kabir back into the room. Don notices Siridevi getting close to Kabir, and he calls out, "Lunch reservation in Hotel Sea Princess at 1.30. Hum late ho jayenge." Siridevi stops him with her hand. She calls out, "Laptop?" Don brings the sleek laptop and places it in front of her face. She turns the screen towards Kabir and a powerpoint presentation starts of the same face of Kabir cut and pasted into ads for travel agencies, resorts, health insurance policies, and health supplements. He shines in them all. Siridevi clicks her tongue and flaunts, "See? Do you know how much all this branding will pay us? Any idea?" Siridevi now catches the agitation on Don's body. She in gentle and sweet words snaps back at Don, "My birthday boy..Muahh. Time is on our side, don't you worry."

She brings Kabir to the sofa and begins again, "First you must come to my mistress again my love, you must please her again. These are little twists and turns in life not written in the guidebooks, but everyone has these little turns, they don't speak about. Hai naa? Wait for my call." Kabir looks at Siridevi's eyes, there's something fiercely impenetrable in them. A chill runs down Kabir's spine for the first time and a fear that probably he is walking up a street which if he turns back will be diabolical. Siridevi and those with her will not let him go so easily. She then gently plants a kiss on his cheek and shows something sparkling in her hand. It's a car key. "This, this is what they do for you, for one night only. Now you tell me what you will add to yourself in a month, in a year?" she offers the key to Kabir, and he touches it.

She holds him by his arm, brings him to the rear side of the bungalow and signals Don to open the doors of what seems to be a concealed garage. Once Don has opened the doors what stares back at Kabir is a shining Porsche. Thick in blue and polished, staring back at him. It's him now. Siridevi gently pushes him and signals him to take the key and sit in it. Kabir takes the key hesitantly and opens the door to sit behind the wheels. The car seat, the smell inside the car, and the world from inside the car change everything in Kabir, from disbelief to belief. Fantasy to reality. It feels true to him for the first time that it doesn't matter who made it. There's a success club party going on somewhere on the top of things, he has to be a part of it. It only takes this much. During his night in the strange bed with a woman pushing herself on him, he had one flash of her, as the mask gave away amidst the act. Kabir remembers it clearly. She almost let herself be revealed to take a Selfie with him. And by now it was clear to him that he was not only serving her but exciting, appealing to Horn Head inside the curtained booth who was filling his pleasure circuit.

Siridevi waves at Kabir, it's a sign for him to drive away. Without waiting for a moment Kabir, reminded of the tiny red plastic car he bought from the Dhulishor fair drives away laughing like a child. He waves at her, at her grumpy Don, and drives away. The lightness of being hits him as he rolls into the street. He takes a long winding road back home knowing he needs to be here, in this moment once and for all. Nothing bothers him anymore, no voices to call him back. He is in sync with the times, the beat. His mind stretches to ideas, and visions. A large house. Travels to all parts of the world. A long drive in a Porche! Meow Meow takes the social media by storm with every passing second and a whole life ahead to work out every dream and desire of his.

This time when Kabir reaches home, he lets the children run up to see the vehicle. He sees Tanvi seated with Alien and lovingly pulls her by her hand to come and see the car. "Come for a ride na Chachi, you are my heroine naa?" a few moments of temptation visit the ex-ruling queen of the silver screen, but she quickly pulls up her guard. "I have had three at a time, luxury cars at my doorstep. This is yours; you enjoy. I've had my time Baba." After a few minutes as the children climb and crawl and sit in the car one of them in his shrill voice calls out, "bhaiyaa you have a visitor, she is waiting."

Kabir wonders, who could it be now? Apart from Siridevi and her gang, he's lost touch with all old friends and associates unless it's another business proposal or some odd fan. He asks the children to come out, locks the car, and flushes into the lift to slide up to his tiny apartment.

There she stands, from her back he knows it's her. That woman, the one and only Smoldering Eyes. She turns, sensing his gaze on her. He looks at her now long enough to wonder what must be in those eyes. "Ab kyaa?" (Now what is it you want?) he asks, she breaks out of her spell. She appears a little dazed to him, could be under the influence of a few drinks. She quickly takes out a few folded sheets from her handbag and gives them to him. He does not want to engage with her, and wonders what she wants from him. Here and there she keeps landing up. "Whatever this is, I am not changing my position from where I have come and where I am going, is that clear?" Sofi gently nods her head signaling she is in no hurry. She patiently waits for him to open the sheets. They are numbers, data, and flowing indexes that Kabir doesn't follow. "What's all this?" After a few seconds she speaks. "The rising Hits and Likes that go for your song are designed, bots can be purchased, artificial intelligence can make it possible. Make the perception of a song, a film, a book, or break it." Her words hit Kabir like bullets. "They did it to you, you are ruined now. Neither can you look back at who you were cause that will make you very ashamed of what you've become, nor will you be able to swallow this new you, for the longest time you've known in your heart of hearts that true music resonates, true need and love for music resonates. This is not you!!" she wonders if she's impacting him. He remains still, unable to digest so many highs and lows in so little time. "I am not a musician, but the circus is not new to me! I was born into it and my fingers are still dug into it well enough to know what makes needles move. It takes what it takes to arrive Kabir." She begins to walk away; he has nothing to say. But she stops in her tracks, she turns to remind, "If you wake up you do know where to find me, don't you?" Without waiting for his answer, she walks away. Kabir tears the sheets into pieces, in rage. He gets into his apartment to breathe falls on the bed and pass out. The scenes from the night before, the car they thrust upon him, and now the truth of his so-called glory... he can't live with himself. A deep slumber from nowhere crawls all over him and makes him as still as a rock. He falls asleep for twelve hours at a stretch.

When Kabir is up the outside is still dark. He has lost track of time; he checks his phone. It's three in the morning. A terrible headache hammers his head. He makes himself a thick, black coffee and then sits still to listen to the stillness of the hour. The night has not passed by, and dawn has not yet arrived. Sofi's words ring loud in the room. Why does nothing make sense ever since he met her? Her words have left him wanting to look away from the truth or force himself to believe she is wrong, and he is right. He looks at the large photograph of his father and thinks of Sofi. The whole day of recording his song, the media questioning him, the interviews, so it was all like a screenplay being enacted? Was he standing on quicksand? Kabir gets up to look at the long mirror he has set up on his way out. As he stares at himself tears begin to stream down his eyes. It is the feeling of returning to the pit. Of saying to himself finally, he hasn't moved an inch. He's gone further down below.

It occurs to him only now that Meow Meow is not the song he came to sing and stuck to the city for so many years or fought with Anu. As a musician, he knows it's of another type, another frequency, anything but his quality, it's not him. Not right to offer the younger audience this as a gift. He hits the shower and stands under the cold shower. The hot water hits his body like sharp daggers piercing and washing out the tire and toil, cleansing the mud in his soul. More tears flow down his face, tyey merge with the bath water and become one. He emerges from the shower to sit on his bed collected. He then wears fresh clothes and sets out. He takes out the car from the corner he had kept it in and drives away. He calls Siridevi's number, once, twice. He is about to record a voice note saying he is going to leave the car outside her cottage in Aram Nagar and the keys by her door. But the phone rings. Over loud music Siridevi's high voice is heard. "Budday, Don ka budday!! Come, come my Jaanu..hotel Sea Princess". Without wasting another second Kabir shifts the gears and races towards Juhu Tara Rd. Unknown to Kabir, Tanvi keeps a close watch on the boy. She knows something is not right, as it always goes sour in the business of entertainment. At first, it all adds up, and then nothing adds up.

The roads have rash drivers, almost wanting to scratch into the brand-new car. Kabir doesn't give a damn. A sleepless, restless city. Kabir's blood boils in his body as he races through the main gate of Hotel Sea Princess, parks the car recklessly on the porch, and rushes through the lobby.

One of the security guys calls out to him for the keys, he walks away as if he can't hear a thing. The Bar is sea-facing, as Kabir walks through the guests the ocean behind lashes out its waves. It is roaring and asking Kabir where his centre is, and what he will hold on to today. The Bar is dressed in confetti and glittering wall hangings of nude female bodies. 'Meow Meow' screams from every possible sound source. They have converted the Bar into a dance floor, pushing the drinks glasses and bottles to one corner. The floor is thick with transgenders, and gay boys and Don in the centre dances his heart away with a drunk Siridevi throwing away currency notes at him. Upon seeing Kabir there's a unanimous squeal on the floor. Siridevi quickly asks them to stop the music. She takes the mike and begins to slur and say, "And now on my Don's Budday the singer the one and only singer of Meow Meow will perform for us live. He loves us and has come to wish my Don!!"

They all begin to clap. Kabir walks closer to Siridevi. He takes out the data sheets that Sofi had brought and throws them in her face. "I came to tell you that the game is up, and I don't need this". Siridevi who has been aware, alert as a jackal on the roads all these years, instantly knows that Kabir has caught up with them. But she is not interested in saving her skin, in fact, she tears down the sheets and begins to growl, "ek toh chances do, uspe apne chaati pe dance saho. Itnaa bhi tu kamaal nahi Raaja. Meri Medum nahi pasand karti toh tereko mein jooti ke neeche rakhti!! Gaata kuch khaas nahi tu, magar deta accha hai. Kyaa karey??" (Who the hell do you think you are? My mistress likes you which is why I don't look beyond that. But it's your delusion that you think you deserve it all. Who says you sing well? You fuck well, that's the truth!) This infuriates Kabir like no one's business. He races towards Siridevi and slaps her right, left, and centre. Don can't take this; he will pounce with his large muscles on Kabir, but Siridevi stops her. "Ruk jaa Don, aaj tera Happy Budday hai, aaj ke din apne haath gandaa mat kar issey chukar." (Let it be Don, it's your birthday why soil your hands hitting this nobody!) But what Siridevi didn't see coming yet was that Kabir's temper was still rising, the sense of humiliation had shot above his ability to take it. With all his temper, and anger balled up together Kabir pounces on Siridevi. He hits Siridevi to make it clear that he isn't taking it lying low. Just when he is about to turn and walk away a sharp clinking sound surfaces from the floor and a spurt of blood is seen. Siridevi's tooth has fallen off. It's lying on the floor. Kabir begins to laugh with the strange meaningless pleasure of having served her right. His job is done, he pats the fuming Don, puts a paper hat lying close by on his head, and walks away. Siridevi shouts while all those she has invited watch this mayhem, "Now you will burn in hell. You saw my nice side, right? Now wait, I will show you my real side. Just wait and watch."

Her phone rings. Don brings it to her. It's her mistress. Metal Mask.

Metal Mask is high, she is growling. "Siridevi...Saali..where the fuck is he? Did I tell you to get him? Why this delay? Didn't I tell you to get him a car or a bungalow or a new song..whatever..whatever it is that he wants?" Siridevi instead of speaking softly sobs, a bloodstream emits from her mouth. Don pushes her a tissue paper, and as she absorbs the blood in it she speaks, "he broke my tooth Maalkin, he will not come to you, nor sing our songs, he is..." Before Siridevi can finish her words Metal Mask grunts, "Ughh now I am angry, very angry." Siridevi pleads, "Malkin, once more let me try?" Metal Mask roars, "And till then? I sit and stare at my empty bed. Send me your Don, at least send that bastard, right now."

Horn Head now prods out of the curtained booth. It is his turn; he will now plunder the black widow. She is high, full of Meow Meow guzzling out of her nostrils. This is his time to strike. Her pet is on her way, the spineless transgender and her lover, they will take at least an hour. Horn Head comes into the satin bed to pull her fair arms to him. She shirks, she resists his touch almost feeling nothing. It makes him try harder. This time with his powerful arms he holds her from the back and throws her on the soft bed. She begins her stream of abuse. But he isn't affected by that. He continues to thrust his male hardness into her. Her body wriggles like she where being tickled. He tries to be rough; he tries the licks the soft abuses and the hard penetration. Metal Mask hurls more abuses at him until Horn Head is bursting with rage. His eyes are ruddy, defeated hearing he isn't enough, he will never be enough, the other boy was better, the stranger whose eyes did the trick, now she wants only him. It defeats Horn Head, his purpose of first entertaining her with the boys and then himself playing the main part. She has reduced him to a pygmy now. He reaches out for the thick candlestand by the bed. He pulls it down and clubs it on Metal Mask's head over and over again. She yells in pain and wants to be rescued; her faithful transgender who supplies young boys is still not there. The dashing continues until Horn Head hears no more sounds from her. She lies there, her mask pushed away, blood streaming into the bed. He realizes she is dead now, cold meat. Meat that will tarnish in a few hours, flesh that will not want warmth anymore. Minutes pass by. It slowly occurs to Horn Head what hes justy done. And now that she is gone, he finds this lonliness unbearable. He throws the candlestand on the floor and sits on the floor to sit and wait and weep softly.

The sky crackles aloud. Kabir has left the Sea Princess hotel. As it rains, he walks past the beach recklessly. The beach is completely deserted at this hour. He walks with the waves hitting his toes, one or two unruly waves lashing against his shin. Their sounds open his pores. At a distance, he can see the tall and widespread property of the Marriott. That is where his feet take him, his being calls out to someone who might be there.

Once in closest proximity of the hotel property Kabir, who knows all the entry and exit points of the hotel aims for the beachside gate which only opens at 7 am. He quickly checks his phone and types Mariott. All the staff security and kitchen personnel appear on his phone list. He calls Bhisham knowing the boy usually has night duty at the coffee shop. The boy whispers, "The night manager is sitting in the lobby, am coming to the beach gate." Within seconds Kabir prods into the darkened corner of the plush lobby. Bhisham squeezes himself into the dark bakery and brings Kabir in. Kabir looks at the CCTV footage in the darkness. Bhisham asks, "Is this the lady you are talking about?" Kabir sees her seated in the coffee shop almost an hour back as the elderly gentleman drinks away. Her eyes are concealed with large dark glasses, but he knows it's her. Smoldering Eyes. He nods, Bhisham looks at him gravely, "wo to martaa hai aadmi isko, sabke saamney. Pati hai." (That man is her husband; he hits her in public.) A helpless rage flares in Kabir hearing that her husband hits her. He looks at Bhisham who by now knows what Kabir wants. He says, "Penthouse 909. Magar Bhaai, aadmi badaa dangerous hai." (You should not go anywhere close to that man.) Kabir is fixed on Smoldering Eyes in the tiny TV screen reflecting the footage from some time back, "ye kaha milegi?" (where do I find her?) Bhisham looks up at the coffee shop and signals towards a corner where the man is sitting and drinking. She sits with her back towards Kabir. He knows it's her.

Kabir gets up to slide past a few pillars and come as close as he can to their table. The grumbling man wants her to go up to her room and wait for him. He is going away to Poona, she is urging him to take her along, she fears being by herself. But he growls, her fear doesn't matter, her desire lessness towards sex at four in the morning doesn't matter, his being drunk and high should not matter to her at all. She picks herself up and moves in the direction of the escalators. Kabir stealthily follows her knowing the man will take a little more time to get up and come to their penthouse. As soon as the elevator stops and it opens, she walks in. Kabir jumps in, it takes her by surprise almost emitting a sound from her shock. As the lift moves up Sofi pleads, "Why are you here? What do you think you are doing? My husband will... if he sees you, he will call the police. Please go away. You must stay away from me" Kabir without a word spoken hugs her. She can feel an electricity generated between their bodies; she must not look away from it. She tries to push him away knowing they are almost about to reach the ninth floor. Kabir mumbles, "I will do something to myself if you don't hold me, I will die, just let me hold you please." The bell clinks as the elevator stops at 9. Kabir stretches his hand to press one of the buttons not aware of where it is going. The elevator now begins to race toward the basement, he holds Sofi close to kiss her, but she doesn't respond. They now glide up again to nine and finally, when the doors open Sofi requests him to stay back. But he follows her, unable to move away from her shade, he walks side by side up to her room.

"He will be here any minute, go." Sofi is aware of the CCTV cameras in the corridor, she knows there is someone watching her. A glazing gaze of someone on her back. But Kabir follows her. With a shivering hand, she runs the room key card on the thick door. It opens to a plush Suite with a tousled bed and the smell of alcohol. Her clothes and things are in a pile in a section. The large glass windows look out into the wild, untamed ocean. Sofi is unable to hold herself back anymore. She holds Kabir by his collar and brings him into the Suite. She is possessed by a strange rush of emotions. She kisses him while holding her close. A rare sense of being alive visits her for the first time in years. They hold each other in each other's arms until the ting tong happens at the door. He is here, she knows his breath. Kabir looks around, almost as if wanting to hop onto the next terrace. The beast is in his childish form calling out, singing out to her, "Baby doll, my baby doll, let me in. Knock, knock, knock dear Beauty, your Beast is here. Won't you open?" Sofi's heart is beating fast. She knows Kamal has an extra room key card; he will snap it any moment now. Kabir sees the row of wardrobes staring at him. The main door opens, and Kamal is standing at the door staring at her. Sofi knows Kabir must be visible to Kamal now as he quickly enters and closes the door behind him. That is the end of them, of Kabir. He can do anything to the boy. But as Kamal sees her in her same clothes and the bed in the same shape, he is furious. Sofi stares at the row of wardrobes standing still, she knows Kabir is there almost feeling his breath on her. Kamal now starts his row of abuses, "You slut, all you need to do is keep the bed, the room ready and open your legs. Why must I spend so much on a slut who doesn't even get her bed ready to be fucked?" Kabir in the wardrobe clenches his jaws, he wonders why he is calling her his slut. Is not Sofi his wife?

About a few slaps and thrashes and kicks later when the body of Sofi has slumped on the floor, Kamal clenches his jaws to remind her, "I am your destiny, your God, your creator, always remember that and to please your God is your only motto of life. Today you have failed, maybe one more chance until I am back." As he turns and rages out, before pulling the door behind him he calls out, "Poona stay extended by two days, then I am back. This place should look polished, I hate dirt or creases." As soon as the main door thumps and closes leaving back a resilient silence, Kabir crawls out of the wardrobe. He comes up to the slumped body of Sofi and holds her close. Her shivering body melts at his touch, his very proximity. On the floor they lie, as dawn lights up the room. On the thick carpet, they make love tender and without words. She was letting air rush into her lungs after centuries of staying parched, every pore of her being, and Kabir too felt alive after so long. It smells like the sodden red earth of his village, like the tunes his Baba played on the Dotara while composing a new song, it feels like the lines in between were erased, on a time machine he arrived in her arms.

At the Madh villa late in the morning the transgender arrives with her birthday boy reeking of cologne, ready to be taken to her, black widow's bed. A sight of torment to watch her boy being devoured by her mistress and yet her mistress Siridevi would do anything, she could not get the boy with the deep eyes. But as they make their way to the pit, Siridevi is devastated to see Horn Head sit at the bedside like a tired beast waiting to be taken care of. Siridevi knows at once what's happened here, her head as sharp as a razor now decides to make a plan while knowing the commissions will stop coming as the lady who asked for pleasure is dead. Then? It's either a lottery ticket now or never.

It takes her an hour to bring a body bag, and fold the now stiffened, cold body into it. And then it must be thrown, dumped. But Don whispers, "You cannot make her disappear. She is Latika Mehta. Her husband is none other than..." Siridevi silences Don as she is thinking again giving odd looks at Horn Head as he has now slumped on a thick sofa. She thinks the story afresh, to tell what must have happened to her own, friends and family, and the police. The gap in her mouth from where her tooth ejected itself pains, the raw wound is alive. Black Widow was with close friends in a closed place until something went sour and one of them happened to hit her and there, the pain in her mouth and the death suddenly became one. Her head rests knowing it has got what it was looking for. She quickly instructs Don to pull out the body bag into their car. Leaving Horn Head to his woes.

Kabir and Sofi lie in each other's arms. He softly asks, "he is not your husband, doesn't seem to be a boyfriend. Why are you here? Come with me." Sofi gets up to turn on the electric kettle and sets up two white mugs. With restless hands, she neatens the bed, clears out the creases on the bedspread, and runs her hands on the carpet. The kettle is ready with the stream blowing out, she cuts two coffee pouches and pours each into the mugs. As the thick coffee smells smear their beings, she sits by him on the floor and smiles to say, "Please don't imagine anyone has forced me to own up to this life. I want all of this, the bed, the lifestyle, these clothes, and my skin, to look at me. In a month I will contest for the Grand Pageant in China. And then my face…" Kabir holds her hand, "No, this can't be your life, this price you are paying is not worth you, don't you know you deserve much more than this?" Sofi is devastated by the truth Kabir brings into the room and yet she chooses to let it go by. Too much is at stake now, it's not a good time to be in love. She sips her coffee softly, pushes Kabir to drink his, then gently smiles and asks, "Let all that be, we were only meant for this much. Now you tell me how do I hold on to you? Your voice..just give me one song. And after this coffee and that song, I will never ask for you again!!"

Kabir is devastated, is Sofi already pushing him back now and forever? He kisses her deeply then promises, "I will bring you a song you will be so..so proud of. Only for you, I will sing. But never talk about partings, never." Sofi thinks of something and gets up. She takes out a leather pouch from her large tote bag and pulls out a thick bundle of Rupees Two Thousand. There must be at least twenty of them. "Here, book a good studio and record your song?" Kabir stares at the money in disgust, he would have truly been helped but he takes it from her hand and throws it at a distance. As Kabir gets up to walk away, he stops to look back one last time and speaks for himself, "You've got tainted living in this world with this man where you only understand everything as a transaction. But my music for you is not a transaction, all I will ever need is your love. You will get your song."

Kabir calls Sunny, "Kahaa mar gayaa Saala?" (Where the hell are you bastard?) Sunny responds, "Just got a new job with great difficulty Bhaai, here near Mhada colony. Can I call you back later? Nayi Naukri hai." (It's a new job) He is about to cut the call, but Kabir calls out persistent, "I need to record a song. It's urgent. In this large, empty city I know you are the only one I can trust. Bhaai, help me with this." His urgency reaches the young and ambitious Sunny. He checks the large wall clock above his head and says, "Can you come right now? My next session is in two hours. Would have slept, I will tell them there's some sound design work going on. Let me turn off the CCTV cameras. Come just now." Kabir is thrilled. He races into the morning air and amidst the drizzle races in an auto towards Mhaada colony.

Kabir sings his soul out, one line after another, all tied into one song. A song of longing, of praising the eternal pain of falling in love that lets the beloved neither rest nor stir, neither breathe nor die. Sunny stares at Kabir as he sings away. In the past few years, he has been with Kabir in restaurants, Bars, and events, and while Anu was not watching) at the over-crowded five-star hotel coffee shops. But today he is singing from somewhere else. Something has taken over him. His eyes glisten with joy and hope, it finally seems like Kabir might present this as the pilot song to any great studio and eventually cut an album. As the music track continues Kabir races out of the thick recording room and comes to sit beside Sunny. To hear the recording, to hear his voice. Sunny plays it and sees him closely, "are you in love Bhaai?" Kabir looks away, he can't tell who it is, he has to stay silent and gift her this song as early as can be though his heart reaches out and wants to tell Sunny a yes. The two met five years back when they were starting, often catching up on the Versova beach with who progressed how much. Kabir nods away his thoughts forcefully, "naa nothing like that, you tell me when do you give it to me? I need to send it right away." Sunny stares at the large TV screen above his head, then looks down at the console and the pile of work in his head. He gently says, "There's lots to finish, but I can always fall sick!!" The boys wink and clap each other's hands in a high five, Kabir is thrilled. As he glides out Sunny calls out, "By tomorrow dawn the song will be on your phone Bhaai."

After a night and day has passed by in the Madh villa the cold body is brought out of the ice slabs Siridevi had placed over and under it. She needed time to pass by, and let her dispersed thoughts come to a still so she could organize the crime well. A thorough round of the highway had to be made to ensure the loopholes were right in place, the spot, the timing. Everything has to be precise to backtrack and place the murder and the murderer in their heads. Her husband will dig up the earth to make someone pay for this fuck up when he finds out.

The Coastal Highway is fully deserted in the morning. There is a section around the corner that has no CCTV surveillance, very few know about this. A car races to stop at the corner. The car door from the back opens for a quick few seconds, it throws out something. Within seconds the car races away. It has dumped the body of Latika Mehta, its head smashed badly, the blood pasted all over its face, frozen for over twelve hours. Within seconds a patrol car doing the rounds notices the body lying by the roadside. The alert calls ring as soon as the smashed face is identified by the patrolling officer.

Inspector Rohan Shinde is still, staring at the piles and piles of evidence gathered on his table from a recent murder but not opening any of it yet. He isn't able to touch any of the witnesses or question them like he would want to do the same. He is about to go home and sleep for two hours, but the phone rings. The patrol jeep blares, it is one of his most dependable assistants, Sule. "Sir, hum Coastal Highway juncture 789 per hai, laash mili hai. 200 percent Celebrity hai Sir, wife of music baron Devang Mehta." Rohan doesn't react much to the last part of the sentence.

By the time he arrives, the area has been cordoned off and guarded though locals hang from all possible tree branches, wall boundary, and ups and downs of the land. Rohan makes his way through the crowd as Sule shows him the site. What is staring at him is the dashed brain of Latika Mehta, the young and sassy wife of the owner of the music company Waves Music. Sule an addict of social media whispers, "Sir power couple of today, Devang Mehta inheritor of his family's four generations old music brand Waves Music, this is his one and only wife. She used to host parties and entertain the industry. So many events and Sir I've heard that..." Rohan now stops Sule as the gossip aunty in Sule seems unstoppable.

Latika's stone eyes look out into the road, a thick velvet gown she must have purchased with a lot of care adorns her body, though the position in which she is lying looks mighty dance-like. A forensics officer steps forward seeing Rohan. "We will send you reports as soon as body leaves from here Sir..but" his words hang in the air as a plush steel grey Rolls Royce comes to a screeching halt close by. As soon as the person seated in the back seat gets off the media hidden amidst the crowd, behind the trees now throng in the same direction. Rohan mumbles an abuse, and Sule's eyes light up. In an austere business suit and thick dark glasses, Devang Mehta rushes towards the cordoned area. The media pour on him, the crowd flash their mobiles to take pictures. He is clueless, lost, and in shock of the fact that it's his wife. In the pressure of the crowd and the police not being able to keep them off him, he passes out. The lines marked by the forensics have been erased. Rohan and Sule take charge. Devang needs to be taken away; the crowd cannot be dispersed. The chances of acquiring prints, or studying the demographics of the place are by now slim to none.

Rohan calmly reflects, "It will take a lot of time to go to Gulmohar as Juhu is a long way from here Mr. Mehta your farmhouse is closer. Can we sit there?" Devang nods a yes. He gets into his car and instructs the driver to lead Rohan's jeep to the villa.

They journey a short distance and enter the sprawling villa. It is a hidden paradise created with a lot of attention and reckless money. As they walk in Rohan eyes Sule, he knows every corner, every inch is to be examined, checked for fingerprints and CCTV footage. But it all looks very neat. As if someone was here minutes ago to leave it spic and span. Devang who must have entered only a few seconds before them enters almost dragging himself nursing a stiff glass of whiskey. With great difficulty, he sits on the sofa, "Yes officer, sorry I needed to make myself a drink. Can we do this fast, please? The whole world's media will descend upon me, it's Latika, my ..." He silences. Rohan takes the cue and nods, "Sure, Sir..did you and your wife.." Devang stops him. "You have no idea about the relationship between me and my wife. Ask my staff, ask my friends and relatives. You know my inheritance in the film industry, I am the fourth generation, and my predecessors were protective about the house. Despite being conservative and very orthodox, I fell in love with her. She had featured in a music video I was producing, and the love was instant. I let her keep our relationship open, the marriage all-permissive." A silence falls in the room, the air conditioners whirr coldly. The term 'open relationship' confuses Rohan. He matches his eyes with Sule. "Open relationship is what Sir?" Devang now explains, "She has..sorry, had a sweet tooth for sex." He looks away letting the words hang in the air. "Since ours is a media-infested world and they are always picking up on our lives, I let her set up these properties, she used to come here with her friends in high places or pick up boys from five-star hotel coffee shops, discotheques and they would have night long, weekend parties. Drugs, money, diamonds, and my Latika amidst all of it." Devang gets up and stands near a picture of him and Latika. Rohan sits and dissects what Devang is throwing at him. "You mean you were okay with your wife sleeping with a younger man?" Devang looks away, at the lawn outside, "I love her very, very much, if she wants younger, macho boys then she wants them. I took care of allowing her enough space and room to indulge. And then what is the use of all this money and influence if you can't fulfill your dear wife's wildest dreams? Yes, I spoilt her, I did. And see now I am getting my punishment. I am a workaholic, I felt guilty for not being around, but I have the burden of success from three generations on my back. Silly girl, don't know whom she made herself vulnerable to, look at me now..." with this Devang breaks into tears. "Who do you think did it to her? Which one of her closest friends or staff? Someone from the inside?" Rohan looks closely into Devang's eyes, "What if I say you did it?" Devang remains still not thrown off by Rohan's mad spree. He gently smiles, "Then arrest me, and yes in a way I did kill her, didn't I? I shouldn't have let her do all this by herself."

Rohan seeing a tissue box close by picks out a tissue to give Devang and gently signals Sule to check the box for prints. While Devang blows his nose Rohan doesn't lose his composure. He asks again, "I don't mean to disrespect you Sir but my eyes spare no one. Do send me the list of people you feel suspicious about. But when was the last time you two met or spoke? Your last contact with her must have been when?" Devang frankly confesses, "the day before yesterday, the 17th I saw her before she was leaving our Pali Hill house". Rohan persists, "Of course, you knew she must be coming to one of your farmhouses, but no contact with her or any staff once she came away?" There's silence. Rohan and Sule eye each other knowing they will only get this much in this round. As Rohan gets up and says the usual, "please don't leave Mumbai without informing me Sir, my card is on your table" Devang lifts his head to think then fishes for his mobile. He takes out his smartphone then scrolls through something and takes out a picture. He stares at it for a second then hesitantly comes up to Rohan to show it "Here, this is from yesterday, this is the last picture she sent me. I don't know who this young man is, but this room is in this villa. But you have to keep this to yourself, my wife's last personal picture cannot be seen by anyone else." Rohan looks at the image of Latika with a strange, crazed look, an odd mask hanging from her chin, and a beautiful young man who is looming behind her quite clueless. He tries asking Devang, but he impatiently produces his hand for a handshake, "I am done Inspector, now I have to take care of everything. And please I want my wife's body for cremation and an answer to who did this to us."

Sofi tosses and turns from side to side on the floor. Her phone plays Kabir's song aloud in the penthouse. It fills her soul with joy, the hope of another life that will never be. She stops the song and calls him as he awaits her response. With a loud beating heart, he picks up her call! "It is stupendous, your voice dearest K." Kabir now knows the purpose has been served, this is all he ever wanted to do and be. Those Smoldering Eyes if they rest on him, he can walk the path ahead. As Sofi talks, she feels an odd fear. She turns as if someone were looking over her from behind her back. But there's nothing, no one but the blankness of her fear. Only that her fears are not false. As they smear, smother each other with love, an intense knowing of each other's presence in the world someone in the hotel is transmitting CCTV footage video to Kamal.

It is the piece where Kabir walks with her into the suite and then it is the footage of him walking out at dawn. Kamal in Poone amidst an international conference, though seated on the stage with a respected panel sees the footage. His gut is boiling, his skin bursting with anger, and he maintains a calm exterior. Sofi continues to look at Kabir with the sun rising behind his back at Kadam Chawl. There's an air of festivity around, it's Holi. They have set up loud sound boxes downstairs and the children are already out in their clothes which after the celebration they will throw away. Women in the building are squealing too while smearing colour on each other. On Kabir's lips there's only one question, "So when can I see you again? Now each song will be a dedication to you. You are my muse, sit in front of me and I will make the best music for you to be proud of?" His doorbell rings. Kabir knows it's the children, he asks Sofi to hold the camera and asks her to be with him. As Kabir opens the door to wish them Happy Holi, he realizes it's not the children. It's a tall man in a crisp white dhoti and kurta and a short, pot-bellied man behind him. They are both unrecognizable to Kabir. He is about to shut the door on them saying they got the wrong door when the man calls out, "Kabir Das? Struggling Singer son of Pobon Das Baul?"

Kabir's stomach drops. He truly does not know these people. Without another word spoken Rohan pushes himself inside the flat. The thin Sule, agile and easy despite his pot belly and wobbly stepping navigates himself to briskly follow Rohan like a shadow and close the door behind them. He looks around, and gazes, Kabir tells Sofi he will call back. The man now calls out, "Crime Investigation officer, Oshiwara Police Chowki, Rohan Shinde." Then turning to his assistant, he says, "Sule!" Sule smiles and is almost about to shake hands with Kabir as anyone related to the case is now a famous person. Rohan thrashes Sule, "he is not some bloody celebrity Sule, I am introducing you to our prime suspect you idiot. Crack kahi ka (you lost your head?) l!!" Kabir is thrown off by the mention of 'prime suspect'. "Hello Sir, what do you want from me?" Rohan is firm, and unapologetic. He pushes back and throws Kabir on his bed. "Devang Mehta? You know?" Kabir knows only the one related to music, the tycoon who absorbs, releases, and is the biggest player in music. He calls out, "Waves Music ka Devang Mehta?" Rohan nods, "his Wifey has tapkaaoed my friend. Rave party, drugs, young boy, sex toy??" The words come close to something in Kabir's consciousness, the setup at that villa in Madh. But he didn't land up on his own there. Siridevi sent him there, he needs to bring that clarity immediately. But before Kabir can say a thing Rohan pulls out his phone. He scrolls through a few photos and then brings the one he took from Devang close to Kabir's eyes. "Now you see? Why we are here amidst your romantic Holi celebrations?"

What stares back at Kabir is the neon-lit room in the basement of the villa, a glaze-eyed Latika looking at the camera, and behind her is a man trying to climb on her. His eyes are glazed too, but that doesn't change the fact that it's Kabir. He begins to sweat. "It's you right my boy? Not a twin brother or some look alike?" Rohan calls out sternly, Sule peers at Kabir's humble abode taking pictures from all angles. Kabir nods and tries explaining, "Sir I did not go there by myself, I went there with..I was sent by... On the 18th..." Rohan asks sternly, "Where were you on the 19th? Between Ten pm and One am?" Kabir has an answer, of course, he was in Sunny's studio, recording the song. For Sofi.

He begins to explain but Rohan stops him. "Not needed here. Come to the Chowki and explain. And if there was someone with you, bring him or her too. Ok, Mr. Toy Boy?" Kabir turns pale. Rohan is ruthless, "abbey apnaa nahi, to apne Baap ka khayal kar leta? Kaisa Banega news item? Pobon Baul ka beta Bambai sheher aake music baron ke biwi ka toy boy ban gayaa?" (If not for yourself you should have thought of your father's reputation. All you ended up being is the toy boy of a music baron's wife?) Sule breaks into an ugly laughter, it impacts Kabir deeply. Rohan then suddenly turns to leave having said what he had come to say, Sule, following on his toes. Rohan stops in his tracks as Kabir tries to speak, "Sir... Sir, I was sent there by someone, Siridevi? The transgender?" Rohan looks at Sule and Sule unable to stop himself, speaks, as the gossip aunty would. He mutters, "Music baron's wife, toy boy, plus transgender..this is a whole prime TV soap, Sahib!" Rohan glares at Sule and with that melts his excitement. Rohan now emphasizes, "Whatever you have in your bag bring it all in, my boy. Tomorrow." As Rohan and Sule leave Kabir hears his heartbeat aloud, his mouth feeling dry and his body feverish. The children rush from nowhere in unrecognizable faces with Gulaal of yellow, pink, and green colour to smear them all over him. "Holi Hai Bhaiyaa!!!"

Sofi sits and listens to Kabir's song over and over until she realizes Kamal has come back earlier than scheduled as her hair almost tears away with him pulling them so hard. She lets out a yell in pain. He picks her up and takes her to the washroom. As he turns on the cold shower Sofi shrivels wondering what's coming up next. He begins to tear apart the loose designer gown she had bought from Hong Kong. He treats her like she where contaminated and then rubs hard on her arms, pinches her nipples to exude a wail of pain, and punches her on her back with his thick arm again and again.

Sofi begins to cry; she knows where this is going. Three years with Kamal had made her aware of his every mood swing and dark temper. He has returned earlier which means something has hastened it and he is not on his mood pills. Now he begins his ugly mutters, "You two-timing whore, how dare you let in another man in my room, fuck him on my bed? How dare you. Did you charge him? How much did you charge now that I have augmented your breasts and made the arch of your nose and cheeks angelic? Huh? Per hour or for a full day?" He now turns off the shower and pulls Sofi back into the room. She tries asking, "What are you talking about?" Kamal is infuriated, "Don't pretend to be innocent you slut, what have I not done for you? And how dare you open your legs for another man? Quickly get dressed and come to the Lounge. I am waiting there for you." Kamal leaves in a huff, Sofi lies in the dry, air-conditioned Suite staring at the ceiling above. Her body is hurting but a clock is ticking as well.

She changes into a fresh velvet gown, wears her makeup as quickly as she can, and steps out of the suite to walk in the direction of the Lounge. She can hear muffled sounds coming from that direction. Her body is alert, her legs shivering. She knows who it is, private investogator Dabolkar. In seconds Sofi is in the Lounge, hesitantly showing herself in knowing the lecherous Dabolkar is devouring her through her gown. Kamal gets up and brings her in to settle opposite the paunchy officer who is unable to stop picking from the array of pastries and Mithaais though his large, yellow teeth are reeking of odour and infection. For a few seconds, they all fall silent. Sofi keeps her eyes lowered; she can feel Kamal's hand move towards him. From nowhere suddenly he then pulls up Sofi's dress. She tries to resist knowing Dabolkar is watching. But Dabolkar sits back, laughing and gazing at them. It's an action they choreographed before bringing her in.

Kamal throws Sofi on the thick sofa and pushing her legs apart thrusts himself into her as wildly as he can. Sofi shuts her eyes, if she had her way, she would block her ears as Dabolkar laughs vulgarly at the randomness of the act. Kamal is heightened in his desire as Dabolkar's laughter gets louder. As Kamal comes closer to ejaculating, he murmurs his abuses, his curses begin to get louder. Dabolkar gets up and comes near the thick glass door of the Lounge to keep a watch, so the sounds catch no passerby's attention. Kamal roars, "You want Dabolkar? Do you want this? There's still enough juice in this pitcher we both can drink from; she called a customer in my absence can you believe that? You two-timing whore?" He slaps Sofi on her cheeks and squeezes her nipples hard until with one thick thrust throwing all his weight on her, he makes it clear that he's come.

After a few seconds, he pulls himself out, picks the tissues on the table to wipe himself clean, pulls up his pants, and smoothens the crease on his shirt like nothing happened. Sofi pulls herself up on the sofa, brings down her dress and keeps her head bent low. She is scared but a part of her heart feels fearless now. Perhaps this is the first flush of love she feels in her body over the years of letting go to Kamal's lust which diidnt stir her an inch. Kabir's song throbbed in her being over Dabolkar's unearthly laughter, over the pains that Kamal inflicted on her. She is now basking in the quiet glow of true love and since those that surround her have never known love, they will never find that secret corner of her. It will always be in hiding, only showing occasional flashes like a voice in her head and heart.

Dabolkar comes back to the sofa and opens his file. The same file, the same papers, the same passport-size photograph of a dark, skinny girl named Vijaya Mishra. Dabolkar places the charge sheet in front of Sofi for whom this should be the final act of making her crush and fall. Dabolkar mutters, "Medam? Do you know her? We all know her, don't we? Why are you daring? What is this daring of yours? Opening shop while sir is away? Please don't do all this, he gives me so much money every month to keep Vijaya Mishra ji in hiding. Don't provoke this large, kind man?" Sofi nods then whimpers, "Actually Sir he was singing in the lobby, I wanted to hear..." an infuriated Kamal gets up, "So you decided to call him to our Suite which is our home? And did he sing and while he sang were you fucking him? Is that your latest kink?" Sofi wonders at this point what if Kamal has a camera inside their room as well? What would he do if he came to know she made love to Kabir?

As her heart pounds louder Kamal pulls Sofi by her arm and throws her at Dabolkar's feet. "Now say sorry, bow and say Sorry Sir, I won't ever, ever look up or speak to anyone else but my master, my God, My creator Dr Kamal Narang. He is the greatest cosmetic surgeon, and he, is the real God, who changes faces, and thus fates of people. Say it all?" Sofi softly repeats every word of Kamal deep inside relieved that he will never know what transpired between them that night. Dabolkar laughs with the pleasure of seeing her at his feet. He gets up and picks up the box of pastries which are heavy with cash. "Okay Dr Saab, until next month then, see you!" Dabolkar flushes out of the Lounge. As if on cue one of the service boys who was instinctively waiting in the corridor sent by the Hotel's management steps in to clear the table.

Kamal holds Sofi by her hand and comes back to the Suite. The regime follows. She stands naked on a stool with little height. She looks straight in the direction of the wall, he uses a thick marker pen to draw indented lines on her nose, on her chin, on the rise and fall of her breasts, and on her hips. Then bringing a sharp scalpel as Sofi shivers, he runs it lightly on his marked lines and mutters, "Better, we will make you better to look at, you are my creation, not some God damned God's. Now that I am creating you with my own hands you will be seen by the world differently. Next month your jawline again. Let's do this nose bridge thing tomorrow, barely two and a half hours job." Tears stream down Sofi's eyes as she is visited by the memory of yet another plastic surgery, yet another month of healing, some tissue torn out of her inner thigh or upper back to put it in the contour of her face, and scars to heal softly. She steps down to look at the still ocean. At the end of the journey, she will be presented at Asia's New Face beauty pageant to be held in China. She will become a catalog for Kamal to show off. Every inch, every part of her will be augmented except for her heart which is still alive, fresh, and beating with longing.

Kabir has waited all day, all night for the Holi madness in the air to die down. It will take a day or so for everything to go back to normal. He keeps calling Sunny but there's no response. His phone is switched off. He decides to check in his studio. At an odd hour. Or even when he lives, in a dormitory facility near seven bungalows. At the studio they say Sunny hasn't come or picked up the phone in two days, they are overbooked and working with a replacement. Kabir rushes to his address but the dormitory with its double bunk beds stares back at him. Nothing is going on here. Kabir is left clueless, staring at the scorching, dusty traffic jam. It feels like a pair of eyes are watching him from the corner of the street, or a van just went by keeping track of his movement. By now they have taken down his song which was only expected. He is back to wondering what about this month's rent, his cards have been frozen. Now there's no Anu to go back to. He walks for a long time until he stops at Versova beach. Though it's hot and blazing Kabir clears his mind giving himself a sense of priority, first he has to get this sticky thing of the Latika murder case inquiry out of his mind. All he needs is Sunny, but why would he disappear? Where to? This is when the thought of Siridevi occurs to him. Why can't he approach Siridevi to tell the police that she had sent him there, to the villa in Madh? And whatever happened, he came back and rejected the offer of the next night which is when the woman died or was killed?

While the beach is getting busier, stalls of food and wares setting up, children playing, again the same feeling visits Kabir, someone watching him as if it were fun to see him sitting staring out at the ocean clueless. His phone rings. It's an unknown number but he picks it up nonetheless anticipating it might be Sunny. It is. Kabir starts with a string of abuses asking why he would keep his phone off and also not be in his dormitory. Sunny explains he was partying with his colleagues, that they had taken off for Alibaugh. The owner of his studio particularly likes him. Kabir realizes something has gone off in Sunny but now there is no time for such introspection, he pursues Sunny being as patient as he can be, "You listen to me, I am in some kind of a mess and my only way out is bringing you to the police chowki and saying on 19th Sept between 10 pm and 1 am I was with you." Sunny listens and gives a wholehearted response to Kabir though he still sounds a little high, "Anything for you Bhaai, anything at all. Tell me where and when I shall be there!" Kabir spells it out as loudly as possible, "Tomorrow 10.30 am we meet outside Oshiwara Police Chowki, and we go inside together. Got it?" Sunny urges Kabir to calm down, "Bhaai, aaram se. It's you, my big brother who was the first person to stand by me when I came to this city with the dream of becoming a sound recordist and someday having my studio. It's you, anything for you." Kabir gently says, "in this strange city Bhaai Things get done only when they get done!" Sunny agrees, and the phone disconnects.

Kabir is relieved for a few minutes at being able to make the connection possible, the normal sights and sounds of the beach now hit him. He sucks in the saline air and his heart yearns for that sweet and sour smell of her nape, a feel of her sweat on his fingertips. He is fiercely missing her, she is this close to him somewhere inside the five-star hotel, in some corner, a spa maybe or the Bar or the swimming pool. This close, he is tempted to rush to the Marriott to have a look at her and gather some strength. As if resounding the state of his heart the phone rings. An unknown number again, Kabir knows it's her. As he picks up the call her words rush in like a warm and foaming gush of ocean wave hitting his skin, "It's me, Sofi." Kabir is wondering if he should confess how closely he has been missing her, hungering for her touch and smells. She calms him down knowing he is about to speak, "Don't speak just listen, don't be seen anywhere near the hotel, don't call on my number. He will go to Breach Candy tomorrow, meet me at the Jehangir Art Gallery around Three, can you?" Kabir makes a little whimper, by then he will have finished with Sunny, and by then his head will clear out again for the plans. The exciting anticipation of meeting Sofi builds. Covering up the anxiety of having to walk into a police chowki for the first time in his life he gurgles out, "Yes, I will be there".

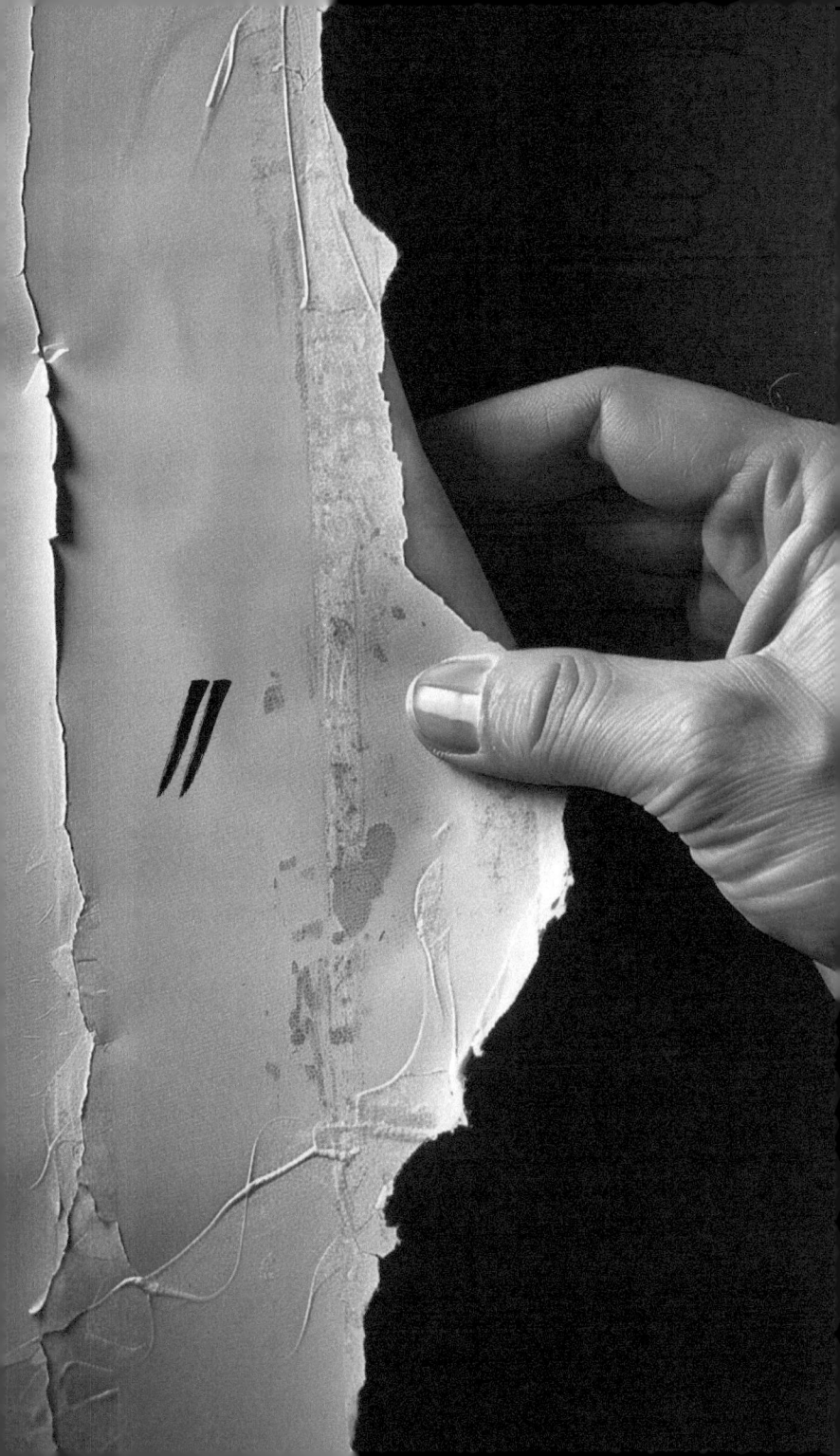

Sunny keeps his word the next day. He appears in front of the police chowki at exactly Ten. Kabir waiting for him guarded by a signpost in a corner comes up to him and hugs him. Sunny is taken aback to see Kabir hassled, his hair ruffled and his eyes tired while Sunny looks unusually well-groomed and clothed. "Wait, Bhaai? Will you tell me what's going on? Why are we going inside? What is my role? If my Studiowaala comes to know I came to the police chowki," With this Sunny makes a signal of his neck being slashed! Kabir looks into Sunny's eyes and asks, "If I say just be with me, don't ask questions, and only say the truth that we were recording in your studio on the night of 19th Sept.? Will you? Can you do just that much? The rest I can tell you once we are out?" Sunny nods. Sunny's phone keeps ringing, and Kabir signals him to put it on silent. Though they are entering the police chowki now Kabir still feels those eyes boring into his back. He turns around to find the dusty, busy New Link Road staring back at him indifferently.

Rohan sits with piles of CCTV footage from various entry and exit points of the Madh villa, Gulmohar building, reports from all departments and the large TV gets blaring about the death of the Waves Music owner Devang Mehta's wife. Conspiracy theories abound, and Sule thrives absorbing all of them. As soon as Sule sees Kabir he mutes the TV and runs up to Rohan asking him to look up, "Arrey Sule, my my, look who is here, Singer Saab!" Kabir stands in front of Rohan with a sense of hidden pride and introduces Sunny. "Sir this is my friend Sunny, we've been struggling in the city for five years together and we have been doing shows on and off. He plays the synth while I sing. He will tell you about the 19th of September night". Rohan indicates that they sit down. He signals Sule to start the recording device while an IT officer comes close to start typing on a dated desktop machine. There's silence in the room for a beat or two, and an aged AC machine continues to whirr.

Kabir wonders why Sunny isn't speaking, he prompts, "Sunny, tell Sir we were recording my song at your studio on the 19th night?" Rohan a seasoned police officer now suddenly barks, "ab uske zubaan mein shabd bhi tu hi dalega?" (You want to put words in his mouth now?) Kabir shuts up. Sunny finally opens his mouth. Calmly he says, "Sir this is true that I have known him for five years, been doing shows on and off. But 19th. Sept? I asked him Sir why he wants me to come here, he didn't say anything." Kabir believes Sunny is cracking one of his ugly jokes. While he is waiting for Sunny to apologise and say the right line Sunny sits back comfortably and waits to be told to leave. Kabir is astounded by Sunny's ease and the lack of need to rectify what he just said, his stomach drops, he begins to sweat, and a slow and soft heartache returns. Rohan comes forward and asks, "So on the night of 19th Sept. you were not with Kabir Das?" Sunny nods from side to side as the IT officer races away typing everything on his laptop. "Sir I haven't met him in quite some time." Sunny says this and gets up, "I have to leave sir, my recordings are all lined up, when we lose a minute in the city, we lose a Rupee or a business account." Rohan looks through a file in front of him where the details of Sunny's studio are registered. Sule matches eyes with Rohan. As Sunny is on his way out, Rohan calls out, "Seems you have just started your studio? Owned by you?" Sunny stutters for a moment, Kabir is astounded by this. Avoiding Kabir's gaze, he defends himself, "We have some property in Dhuliya sir, just sold off everything to make a fresh start." What stares back at Rohan is the details of Sunny's home address with no so-called claims of property transfer or sale.

Then without waiting for another moment Sunny turns and leaves. Kabir who by now has a calculation going on in his head enraged gets up and is about to follow him but Rohan stops him, "Wait! You Chutiya! how dare you waste my time!? You remain seated." Kabir looks helpless and scared. Rohan comes forward, "Why did you bring this boy and waste both his and my time?" Kabir straightens himself up, "Yes exactly Sir, why would I bring him? You are hanging like a sword on my neck, and I would just waste your time? Don't you see he is lying? He's got a new studio, how?" Rohan now sits back and Sule signals the IT officer to leave. "Tell me, tell me why is he lying? Are you the biggest singing talent in the country? Does he have to compete with you?" Kabir persists, "Sir I am being framed for a high-profile murder which I have not committed, it's about very big people, so naturally someone very big is trying to do this." Sayajit now bursts out laughing, "Sule? I always hear you tell me crazy tales about these cinemawaalas, entertainers huh? But crazy like this? What does this city do to common people? Really!" Rohan now gets up and comes close to Kabir. He sits on the edge of the table and bending down matches his eyes with Kabir, "twenty four hours. Go get an alibi, or else without a warrant without anything I will arrest you, and once in..." Rohan turns to look at a file with Kabir's name on it. "Son of renowned Baul singer Pobon Das accused of killing Latika Mehta wife of music baron. The murderer was a toy boy of the deceased." With this Rohan and Sule laugh, Kabir gets up and races out, his skin burning in rage and with silent humiliation tearing down his inner voice.

He has lost track of time. He races in an auto towards Aram Nagar. Now that the friend he counted on has moved on, the only person to reach is Siridevi. Kabir is convinced she must have taken Sunny in her fold. Money, some extra work, anything. It didn't take an extra minute for a car to come and pick up Sunny from the Chowki. And by the time he got dropped off at his new studio, Sunny was heavy with another gym bag full of cash. He will never look back to find out whatever happened to Kabir after this point. After a few moments, Sule whispers into Rohan's ear about the plush car picking up Sunny from outside the Chowki. He nods and returns to the media circus on TV while muttering under his breath, "that poor boy will have to get his alibi now". Sule is filled with admiration for his Boss's insight.

The afternoon is lazy in Aram Nagar, the bungalows occupied with rehearsals, acting workshops, dance classes, ,pilates and exotic training of breathing and mind cleansing. Kabir comes to what he once knew was Siridevi's bungalow. But the entrance, the door he knew was not there anymore. It's all heaped with coconut fronds. Kabir's head spins, he feels tired but restless. There's a Paan Shop close by. Kabir walks up to the shopkeeper attending to his customers. He calls out, "Bungalow 18?" He looks in the direction of the bungalow then gets back to his Paan saying, "This is Andheri Nagri, what you saw yesterday does not exist today, what you see now will be gone tomorrow. Mirage..everything is a mirage." Kabir does not wish to engage with the Paanwaala, he makes his way through the rubbles of Aram Nagar.

Just then his phone rings, and his heart trembles. For Kabir every sound, every sensation is now doubly amplified. He fumbles into his pocket, his fingers cold as ice, and takes out the smartphone. It's Rohan. The same calm and easy tone comes across. "Alibi milaa?" (Did you find an alibi?) Kabir stares at the distorted scape of Aram Nagar looking back at him and helplessly he admits, "No Sir, not yet I came looking for Siridevi. Her dance classes happen here only. In Aram Nagar, but..." Kabir's silence catches up with a restless Rohan. "But..then nothing happens." Kabir tries explaining, "Sir I couldn't have got it so wrong. She has about thirty gay boys who rehearse here, she trains them, and sends them to weddings and other functions. This is her on-the-face income and then she claims to be the agent of one Diamond Music Company which is why she came to my doorstep." Rohan has heard enough of this, he keeps calm and says, "Look Kabir, your friend comes to speak on behalf of you, he turns against you. You go looking for the transgender, she disappears along with her institution. You tell me what it is that you want me to do? I have to answer my department, the media, and above all myself. This is a very high-profile case, and the media has made a circus out of my investigation. Do you realize I am sticking it out for you?" Kabir knows what the earnest cop means. "Yes sir, I know, and I also know that you know I am innocent." Rohan is hit by Kabir's stark confession; truth is visible like wildfire in a forest if not always adding to the right cause at the right time. Kabir continues, "Allow me time till tomorrow morning Sir. I will come to you with an alibi, I will Sir."

As the phone disconnects Kabir is left to the sights and sounds of ordinary Aram Nagar. He thinks hard and tries to focus. He remembers Sofi's call; she would be at the Jehangir Art Gallery. Whatever money he has he calls for an Uber and races towards it. The traffic is slow and yet Kabir doesn't want to give up on this one chance. His phone purrs, and she tells him she has entered the gallery and has very little time on her hands. His Google map shrieks, "Your destination has arrived, it's on your left." Kabir pays the Uber and races into the gallery. Racing through rows and rows of insipid paintings he finally comes and stops where he knows it is Sofi lurking in a corner. He gently touches her shoulder, she turns, and there's a large dressing done across her nose running into her cheek. Her face looks swollen. As viewers exchange notes and stare at paintings the thirsty lovers hug each other. Kabir gently holds Sofi's face; she is in pain. "What has happened to you? Did he again" Sofi rests her finger on his lips, and he silences. She whispers, "It's just one more face correction surgery. This was minor, I just need a couple of days' rest and must avoid dust and pollution. I can't meet you anytime soon, just wanted to tell you this." Sofi holds Kabir close, and they walk away to a deserted corridor that looks out into a large lawn full of trees and the ground abounds with thick grass. Sunlight of the late afternoon pours in through a skylight. She kisses him close and whispers, "he is nearby and will be here any minute. We are buying a painting." Kabir finds it meaningless, the pain, the scars, and the paintings. His eyes brim with tears, he wants to tell her how helpless, how agitated he's been but runs out of all words. They hug silently. Kabir knows it's time to part again. He promises, "The next time we meet I want more time with you, I need you

Sofi." She nods and then shows him the road outside. Kabir knows where he needs to go from here.

As he gets into the cool Uber the vehicle races through the tall, ageless buildings of South Mumbai, a world more like a dream. The ambitious Coastal Road like a dragon's open mouth stares back half-done standing on the ocean. He pulls down the glass window to feel the hot air while they race into the Sea Link bridge. As the sun dips into the horizon, he nears Bandra. The tall building just behind Mehboob Studio stands well protected and guarded by Tiwari ji from Banaras. The man keeps at his Paan, his phone with 'Aaj Kal' news, and keeping to the entry book for every visitor while scanning them with his weathered eyes. The moment he sees Kabir coming near the gate his senses are awake and alive. Kabir walks in but Tiwari realizes things have changed now in the past few days, he has to be stopped. He is a face on all news channels now, they are blaring and deducing loud and clear that he killed the wife of Devang Mehta, the owner of Waves Music.

Anu's house is set up with lights and a camera. A photo shoot happening of a young, macho boy Ankur. She looks into the monitor, only to find him staring back at her as cold as frozen meat. He needs thawing. She clicks her tongue and signals the photographer to wait. She comes up to him, and whispers into his ears something inaudible even to the photographer who is not too far from them. She teases the boy a little pinching into his bronzed flesh, warming him up. She tickles him behind his ear. Anu's fingers and words are magic. For years now she has been handling these hungry, anxious boys and girls who want to make it large in the entertainment world having seen some old copy of Vogue or Femina here and there while living in his small town. While they think the world is waiting to embrace them all that stares back are the harsh tentacles of reality that throttle and push them back as much as they can! Unless they bring something out of them, key into a personal note or element they exude nothing worth luring a reader or audience anyhow bored with his or her life.

Within a few seconds of Anu's personal touch Ankur's look changes. As the clicks rise in the air Anu signals Ankur to keep changing the way he holds his arm or to look at her instead of the camera. This is when the doorbell rings. Anu wonders who it is. Her thick Goanese cook Celine in her grey gown throwing her weight around with her tied-up bleached hair and large frame steps out of the kitchen to go attend to the door. Anu uses the moment to pick her diary to check but she has kept nothing before 4 pm as she knows the photo shoot will wrap up only around Two after which Ankur wants to hang around in the house and learn more from her. She sees that hunger in him which she once saw in Kabir. Though she was about to tell herself that it was all over, no more grooming these small towners, she stepped back upon seeing Ankur. She asked herself, why should she give up on a skill and place she's made for herself in this ruthless town?

The door behind her has opened and there's stupendous silence. Anu turns back to find Kabir standing like a thief at her doorstep. She signals the photographer to take some shots of Ankur while she handles the problem at hand. A wink at the boy from Anu and the constant clicking sound of the camera will keep him on heat. Anu picks up her silver cigarette case and lighter and then lighting one of her slim sticks comes up to the door. She stands in front of Kabir while signaling Celine to leave who has had a soft corner for the boy. While Celine turns away Anu without matching eyes with Kabir mutters a synthetic, slippery, "Yes?" She takes in deep puffs of the cool mint cigarette waiting to end the matter once and for all. Kabir, despite the gaze of the boy in the lights and the photographer giving him odd looks from time to time joins his hands and pleads to speak privately to Anu. Anu nods away indicating she has no time. Kabir mutters, "I am sorry Anu, I bad mouthed you, I said I would never turn back. But..I am in deep danger of getting arrested any minute. I am being framed for a murder I haven't committed. Please help me. I did not do it." Anu now looks back and calls out, "Hey you guys do you know him?" the clicks have stopped, and the thick and heavy lights turned off for a few seconds. The silence in the room is palpable. Anu now speaks, "Yes, your silence speaks for itself. At my doorstep is the suspect in Latika Mehta's murder. Isn't that what you are called on TV and on all social media sites Kabir? And when they churn and turn up your entire history and link you to me, and with that comes my carefully, thoroughly worked towards reputation to a question! Do you know what it takes to set up a reputation in so..so many fucking years in this city? Do you?" Anu's voice suddenly cracks through the silence of the room.

Kabir has no choice but to speak, the innocent can still speak. "Anu, you know I didn't do it, I can't kill a media baron's wife, you know it. Please, I have been at your beck and call for five years. Only one last favour I ask from you, just come with me to the cops and say you were there with me on the 19th night?" Anu loses her calm now, "Lie through my teeth, Kabir? Because you choose another bitch's bed leaving mine?" There is a stone silence where the obvious is known to each one and yet!

Kabir knows his walking away from her has hurt her the most. Anu was always scared of being abandoned, as a child she was left in an orphanage by her unwedded mother. She wanted in Kabir a mate for her years ahead, somehow make -up for the long years of hard work and the relentless task of setting up her brand when she neither rested nor let a relationship grow. She will never come back to where she was or make it an inch easier for him. "I bring you to this city, feed you, clothe you, teach you to walk, talk, give you a bike, money, even a singing opportunity in my private circles, in my events I promote you, even use my contacts to overnight book a trial recording with Darshan Taloja and then? You suddenly leave me out in the cold for no rhyme or reason and now I should come to the cops and say I was fucking you?" By now the surrounding apartments that are usually indifferent and self-absorbed have opened their doors too. Celine has stopped her work in the kitchen, she stands still waiting for the tamasha (drama) at the door to be over. Hasn't the boy had his fair share of humiliation? But she knows Anu won't let this one go. Celine feels guilty, when the intercom rang inside the kitchen and Tiwari said it was Kabir she thought this was the best thing happening now. The boy was sweet and gentle, the house felt so full of life in his presence and he doted on her spicy fish curry and bread pudding. And as a caretaker of Anu, she knew the woman needed a grounded boy like Kabir. Tears stream down Celine's eyes. All Kabir can try is one last 'please' but something stops him. Beyond this point, he cannot ask. He has done this to himself. Anu is bursting in rage. Unable to stop herself she then suddenly pulls at Kabir's shirt, her sharp nails gripping into the fabric making it snap. She tugs at him roughly, a little helplessly. "Goh..go and get help from new friends." Kabir turns away having come full circle in his head, he knows that morning at the Star Studio Anu had set up work for him. Someone snapped the ties, someone who didn't want him to get what he wanted. Who? Vimla again?

As Kabir walks towards the main gate Tiwari the sturdy guard with his phone blaring the latest from the news channel watches him go by. He stares at Kabir's photo on the phone screen and gives a lingering smile. He observes Kabir's walk. The last time he left it didn't feel like he would never return, but this time, Tiwari knows they are now strangers forever. Every day strangers meet in this city like logs of driftwood floating on ice water and come together for a while, floating with the current until the current takes them in different ways. Kabir's currents are thick and heavy.

Kabir walks slowly back until he is close to Juhu. His limbs ache, his head throbs, he feels his parched throat and wants to put an end to punishing himself. When he crosses Marriott he remembers the lingering smell of Sofi's mouth, the arched back of her neck, and drop of her shoulders. Her thick, bleached hair made a clump on his face, its smell mixed with his and their lovemaking. He stops a rickshaw and throws himself into it to just about be able to say, "Veera Desai." The rickshaw man arches his gaze and looks at Kabir. He is a curious old man who begins to talk about the country, and the flags ruling the nation. How he came to Bombay to make money and suddenly one day owned a rickshaw. Kabir says a gentle "hmm..Hmm" in a rhythm to let the old man know he is there, listening, holding his hand in the long lonesome journey ahead. Dusty and broken Veera Desai Road stares back at Kabir. He lets the auto go a little before his lane, takes a sharp turn, and gives the old man a hundred and fifty without bothering to wait for the change. As he crawls back to his abode the city has driven him mad and wild, he wanted something from it, he worked towards it, and yet the essential dream of being a voice, a voice to remember, he couldn't be that.

Kabir nears his building crossing the broken, construction site road but unlike a usual late night when the residents fall asleep as they must prepare for the day ahead, they all seem gathered. The notorious children are in a group at a distance while Tanvi looks wrecked. The elderly are gathered around her while the men in a corner are talking amongst themselves. Kabir races to Tanvi seeing her face drained and deathly pale. "Aunty? What happened?" Tanvi hugs Kabir, her own has come. With Kabir, she shares a bond, a fight, a giggle. She bursts into tears and says, "Alien...Alien hasn't come back." While it gets tough for her to speak one of the elderly women speaks out, "she let him play in the evening and went up as usual. But he never went up today. And there's no sign of him anywhere around." Alien flashes in Kabir's memory, his heart says the boy is being naughty and will be back soon. His weight and own worries overpower everything else. As if everything he sees, touches, and feels has become black, sooty like a bottomless emptiness echoing in his soul.

As he climbs towards his apartment the faces of Sunny, Anu, and Siridevi throb in his head, resounding like a gong saying this is what it is, this is what human faces are. Sofi's scarred face looms large. The night of violet vapour, the scent of the woman who first appeared in a metallic mask and later turned out to be Latika lying on the highway amidst a forest, visits him, her lustful moans. She must have shrieked in pain when they killed her, whoever. Was it them or one person? He drags his body like a lead down the corridor of his apartment. It feels like the walls marked with crayons, pencil scratches, and beetle juice spurts are closing on him, so much pain, tears, and dissolution abound. With all his might and effort Kabir turns the key to enter his apartment. Finally, to breathe for a little while.

The darkness echoes with silence but a stench overpours everything. A dead rat? He smells it and feels like it is the stench of his failure, of his doom crawling up to him as the clock ticks to usher in a tomorrow when he will not have an alibi and need to walk into the hands of law, when once and for all the darkness of oblivion will fall upon him. But while thoughts disappear, mood scapes change the stench gets stronger forcing Kabir to turn on the light near the door. What he stares at he couldn't be mistaken by, even if it is at a distance. He has loved and played with that body, its furs and affection still sit like a layer in his being. What stares at Kabir is the stabbed body of Alien. A stream of blood had flown towards the door as if it were calling out, claiming his breath. Kabir quickly switches on all the lights in the house. There is death at hand. Of a creature that must have helplessly squealed. His Baba used to do this. The night his mother died they stayed up, set up lamps, and turned on the lights in the village till dawn until when she was cremated. And as all the lights come on Kabir stares at the wall in front of him. On the wall written in Alien's blood is clear, "Aglaa Tu". (You are next.)

Kabir feels like his breath is shortening, his vision blurring. The voices and visions in his own head, tire, hunger, and the oppressive smell of death lying inches away from him shriek and beat him. His body slumps on the cold floor and Kabir passes out unable to call out for Tanvi or reach his phone for help. After long Kabir's eyes open. The room is still very dark, it must be almost Two in the morning. He looks around his room, and then at Pobon's large photo looming over his head. He gets up with great difficulty and touches Pobon's photo. Kabir knows he has to leave and run away from an invisible pair of hands trying to throttle his neck. He can't go back to his village as it will affect Pobon too. He reaches out to a drawer close by and picks up whatever cash is lying there. And a debit card that still has some money, his passport, and all ID cards. Kabir is all set to leave. He has to leave without a trace, so the invisible hands don't make a ruckus with these innocent people living here.

Kabir softly knocks on Tanvi's door who sits on her tiny cot crazed, waiting for her pet while the animal lies cold in the next apartment. Kabir holds Tanvi by her hand and gently brings her to his house. While she can't believe what lies before her and is too dumbstruck to emit a voice he whispers gently in her ears, "he is gone from us now Chaaci. And I will disappear too if I don't run". Tanvi breaks into tears but holds Kabir close knowing this might be the last time she's seeing him. As Tanvi tries her best to cope with the two-fold tragedy of Alien's death and Kabir racing against time, she curses the city. In the darkness Kabir melts, unaware, and undecided about where to go. But he won't look back at this city. Maybe he will take a train to a town close by or a bus to somewhere, some stoppage, and sit quietly for some time. Let them find out who it is that killed Latika, let them find out the meaning of all of this. Only if he ejects himself maybe they will try and find another link, possibility, clue into things. But Kabir doesn't know truly where he will go. Her 'Smoldering Eyes' burn in him, one last flash of them, a need, a response, just one contact with her. He tries to stop himself but finds himself incapable of passing by the Marriott. Just that one last time!

The large room is hung on weed smoke. Empty glasses of whiskey abound on the side table. Kamal sleeps like a beast put to rest on a spell. Sofi is lying still under the weight of his thick, boxy arms claiming their space with her even when he is sleeping, her scar still needing repair plastered thick. She hears her phone gently purr, her senses are alive, awake, and raw. A scar runs through her nose, the nerves are raw, and her face is swollen. Her head throbs in pain, the medicines that Kamal gives her in red, pink, and yellow which she knows will leave her open to him and blocked out of herself she tucks in her secret compartment behind the side table. Pain keeps her alive, the raw pain and the ticking of the clock one second after another. Without stirring a fiber in Kamal's body Sofi slips out her hand to stretch and reach her phone. She knows the number; she looks at Kamal as the cold phone keeps purring in her hand. She is visited by a pain deep down in her being somewhere that can't be held or described or named. Pain makes her fearful, the present pain is better than the imagined one possible ahead of her. She is guided by her pain and told to shut off the phone, gently she taps it off and keeps it back on the table. A few seconds pass by, the outside is silent with an occasional heavy vehicle passing by which doesn't reach past the thick glasses and walls of the penthouse. The clock in her mind ticks, and Kamal growls in his sleep. Her phone begins to purr again as if drawing her in with his hot mouth. Making the pores in her body open and aware. It's hungering for him.

Once inside the large washroom which by rule she has to keep open at all times when she is using it, she pushes herself to a location away from the mirror so that even if Kamal wakes up to piss the first thing, he doesn't see is her on the phone staring back at him from the bathroom mirror. She whispers in the gentlest voice, "But I can't meet you. You saw me, didn't you? This is my life, stitches, and scars until I get the perfect face and stand before the world. We will never be together. Not now, not ever, we are over. Something happened, it happened like it happens to thousands of people in the world and then it falls off. Let this be The End, please." Sofi hears Kabir's silent tears standing in the cold stone bathroom, the freezing vent of the air conditioner blowing into her bones. She whispers after a few seconds, "thik hai..one last time, behind the lobby there's a concealed lady's washroom, farthest away from the café?"

In a deserted hotel lobby where all is still, the bonsaied plant tubs and flower arrangements nod at each other silent for some time now. A pesky receptionist is fighting with her husband on the phone, and the Sardar guards at the gate are handling their overnight duties. They are removing the croissants and brownies from the glass shelves so they can fill them up again at dawn. Kabir slides into the restroom. It's by and large deserted, a young girl in a neon pink dress is puking at a wash basin. Her silver pouch pouring out pouches of Meow Meow sparkles in the semi-darkness, Kabir passes her by wondering where Sofi is. And then suddenly from nowhere, a hand emerges to pull him in. There she is with a thicker white tape at an angle across her nose. In a silken gown the colour of her flesh almost. Her hair is clumped up to the top with a few loose strands lashing out. He holds her close and feels angry, very angry for not having been able to overcome this. This woman this feeling, this moment. If he only knew why. He runs his hand on the tape across her nose, behind which hides the scar he had last seen, but it seems to have swollen, and gone into an infection. A gentle river of tears flows down her eyes, she is drawn to him, and he is to her. He kisses her hot mouth, and a loud talk starts outside. A woman and his husband's girlfriend are shouting at each other. They fight over who gets how much out of the man they each have a share of. The sounds of sandals, stilettoes, and boots abound, the wash basins flush water and stop, and the cisterns gush out water into other cubicles. The abuses rise, the water sounds clamor around them, and the heat between Sofi and Kabir rises. Shuffling in the tiny space, melting into each other's heat, they make wild love like there will be no tomorrow.

Strangers outside continue to merge and mingle, urinate, fart, abuse, take pictures of themselves, spray thick perfumes, dispose of used sanitary napkins while Kabir and Sofi sit locked close as if they were pasted into each other's beings. He then softly whispers, "Now I can die. I am going away. Forever leaving this city. Wanted to see you only once, this once." Sofi's spell breaks with those words, like he had suddenly turned into a ghost. She couldn't believe her ears. She gets up immediately and unlocking the door of the cubicle steps out. The large bathroom was sprinkled with women of all shapes and sizes.

Seeing her emerge and Kabir following her they disperse immediately. She stands in her bare feet silken gown and undone hair staring at Kabir in disbelief. "What did you just say? What level of a coward are you? Don't you understand the meaning of freedom? You are on the other side! You can sing, your voice is like nectar, you came here to share your voice with the world but now you want to go away? What kind of madness do you so-called normal people practice?" Kabir emerges to hold her close. He says it all, "I am being framed, someone, somewhere wants to get me for a murder I did not commit." Sofi hears this but no is not an answer she will accept. She thinks, her eyes blankly looking above Kabir. A few seconds pass and then she tells him, "Stop, wait, let me think. I have a solution. You need a lawyer, not a good but a great lawyer. I know a guy, he once gave me his card, I met him at a party Kamal took me to, and within seconds he knew I might need to reach out for help." Kabir looks into her eyes lost, molten, mesmerized. His gears have shifted inside, he knows he wants to do this only for her, let her hold his hand and take her ahead.

At sharp Ten, Kabir enters the police chowki. Rohan, busy amidst papers and files and all kinds of calls coming in from all kinds of departments signals Sule to attend to Kabir. Sule guides him and they enter a chamber. Kabir finds someone waiting on this side of the table. As soon as they enter the gentleman gets up and turns to register Kabir. He stretches out his hand and says, "Kabir? I am Irfan Merchant. Sofi's friend." Kabir nods, shakes hands, and settles down beside him while Sule ejects. In the cool silence of the room, he holds Kabir's hand and mutters, "You don't worry, you will not be accused of something you haven't done." Kabir nods and Rohan enters. As he settles down, he is taken aback to find Irfan seated beside Kabir.

"What brings you here my capable and successful lawyer friend?" asks Rohan curtly. Irfan leans forward to speak humbly, "All cannot be for money Rohan, you and I have had enough of our differences. Now I am here to support my trapped and innocent friend who has not committed a crime you accuse him of. You know it, he is one of those unheard, unseen faces who sucks up the dust of this city hoping to be seen somewhere or heard in a music video on YouTube someday. How can he kill Latika Mehta?" There is silent eye contact between old friends, a memory of clashing swords in a case, of ethics vs the truth. They had parted ways here, Irfan defended a case because of the money and fame, and Rohan knew he was letting the wrong guy out. Despite having been from the same school and university they had parted, praying they never have to meet again. Rohan maintains his steel like exterior, "All I asked for from your client Mr. Merchant is an alibi. You understand alibi, don't you? Someone who can say on the night of Latika Mehta's murder he was doing this or that with that person?" Silence falls as the truth is the need has not been fulfilled by Kabir so far.

Irfan nods, then gathering himself asks, "Have you heard about the Mehtas not being in the best of relationships with each other? A colleague says they were each separately weighing the pros and cons of the marriage. What about that? How about the intent of murder being pointed somewhere else?" After a brief moment of silence, Rohan now signals Sule. Sule brings in an IT officer who comes with his laptop. Rohan signals him to place it in front of Irfan and Kabir. The officer positions it correctly and plays a video. It is a CCTV grainy footage. The date on the screen shows the 19th. Sept. The night of Latika's murder. While everything looks still at the front gate of the villa in Madh after a while the gate opens to let out someone. As the person walks out, he is more visible. It's Kabir, shirtless, glaze eyed. He and Irfan share a look. Kabir mutters, "This must be from the 17th early morning after they threw me out. It must be! Sir, they have changed the dates surely. This is from that night I went there." A long pause falls into the space until Rohan gathers himself and continues, "Now tell me Irfan what am I left with? No choice but to arrest him. Can you imagine the pressures on us? Devang Mehta's wife for fucks sake!! I am the one making my case more and more visible, questioning every single house staff, employee, and hopeful, their collegues, have- been stars, while making my way through the media of the whole world descended on us and now you are telling us how to do our job? Every day there's a media trial, they pick up Judges, lawyers, and senior journalists and start a ruckus. Right now, the nation is waiting for the media to tell them what happened to Latika Mehta. We are serving them." There's a palpable silence now in the room. Until Kabir speaks out, "Sir I am being framed, to put it on me suits someone. Someone out there." Rohan is infuriated by this, "Who?" he tries to understand. "Tell me, if you are a 'maamuli' struggler in this city like lakhs, crores of cockroaches eating, breathing, sleeping occupying a corner in this city then why would someone be after you?" Irfan now steps in and bursts out, "kyuke ye ginti mein nahi aate" (because they don't count). Irfan and Rohan exchange a look and a wall breaks. Rohan is fast thinking of something. He then comes up with a plan. "Okay we will let you go, if someone is framing you then they will follow you, get to you, and do something. Let's see!" Kabir and Irfan get up with the resolve of coming back with an alibi. Rohan looks away waiting for them to leave, unable to gather his emotions after having brought the ever arrogant, commercially successful Irfan on the same page for once.

Kabir thanks Irfan for his support, he says goodbye to him and takes a turn. For the first time, it feels like hope cannot be abandoned, a chance to exhale easily will soon come. As Kabir turns the corner and walks ahead the feeling of a breath, a gaze on him doesn't escape. He stops and turns back to find the lane empty. There's now very little money left with him. The only blessing of his parents in the form of a gold chain is gone, there's nothing more the city can take away from him but this body that has a voice, a voice bursting through its seams. Kabir walks two steps again, the breath follows, he stops, and the breath stops. Is he going mad? Just when he is about to take a step again a sharp object strikes him in his head. A few seconds of blindness follow until he finds himself inside a plush car with a thick smell that reminds him of someone.

A heavy-structured man sits in the back seat beside him. A purple stone in a gold ring sparkles in the darkness. It's Kamal, he is nursing a whiskey and scratching his grey beard. The smell is of Sofi, a sweet sap and a divine freshness, the perfume she uses. Kamal gets to be this close to her all the time, he is the benevolent benefactor, the giver of the promised life which Sofi thinks is the only way to be. But Kabir knows, to him she is nothing more than a slave. What could he now want from Kabir?

Kabir's head is still hurting. As his senses return to him it is only now that Kabir registers in the darkness a sturdy investigator in the front seat with a thick stick in his hand. This is what he must have been hit by. From there came that blunt, sharp pain still gnawing from his seams. "What do you want from me? I have nothing to offer, what am I doing here?" He is met with silence on both ends. Kamal picks up his glass and continues to sip. Dabolkar goes first, "If you would have just one 'Kaand' (episode) my dear honest and earnest citizen!! From one kaand you have now just rolled into another." Kabir is further confused. Now Kamal takes charge, he sits up and pushes the whiskey glass to Dabolkar who is shy at first but later grabs it.

As Dabolkar takes large gulps even before Kabir can pre-empt what's coming up Kamal uses his large, rough hand and slaps Kabir tight. Another one, another. Tears flow with the raw pain making his skin burn. Kamal growls, "How dare you touch her with these hands of yours, how dare you? I have created her, and given her everything, I am her only source of life and sustenance. Do you know who she was? Have you seen her for real?" Kamal now picks up the weathered file of Sofi from the shelf on his door and throws it at Kabir. It's the same file from the police records that Dabolkar always waves at Sofi when she behaves like a disobedient child and reminds her of the obvious fate in a prison as opposed to basking under the spotlight of fame. The file contains the passport-size photo of a dark, blank-looking girl staring back at him. The name says, Vijaya Mishra. It is the eyes of this most bland girl. Her eyes get Kabir questioning, he's seen them before.

"This is who she was and was sitting in jail for having injured someone in a road accident in Nagpur. All she wanted was to be free, free at the cost of anything. Do you understand anything? This Dabolkar used his network and helped her come out, he designed a Parole and then my hands!!" Kabir stares at Sofi's old photograph in disbelief. As he looks at her greasy, bewildered self and secretly knows he would even love this girl if he met her accidentally Kamal continues, "she wants The Life, my boy. The Life! Have you seen what I have given her? The bags? Shoes? Her new face!! I have left my stamp on her body, so you have more reasons than one to step back." As Kamal talks of the things he has given her, Kabir is visited by the day he hid in the wardrobe and watched him ravage her. Every slap, every push, every plundering, and her silent sobs. And yet the bags and shoes and perfumes are necessary for her. She wants them as much as she wants a taste of that love she tasted in his mouth and his smell. Her skin and sweat are alive and throbbing in Kabir making the threats of Kamal sound empty, he is pushing Kabir away feeling as insecure as a schoolboy. Kabir remains quiet, waiting for Kamal to end. After he has finished his speech and when Kamal thinks the impact has been made Kabir sits staring at the back of the seat in front of him, he claims calmly, "My love is not a lie, neither is her love for me going away too easily. Now you do what you need to do." This quiet resolve of Kabir sets Kamal mad. His rage bursts through his seams, he growls. He punches Kabir until his nose bleeds and Dabolkar whimpers. Dabolkar calls out, "Sir, Sir, beat but with love! Now if this boy goes and files a complaint." Kamal is deaf to Dabolkar's words knowing Kabir is already under the radar, fleeing from second to second. This is his only chance. After a while when Kamal is done more than enough, he bends forward to open Kabir's side of the door. Kabir's hurt, sapped body slides out of the car and falls on the dusty ground. The car races ahead into the dust.

On the deserted alley, Kabir lies still. Lightly breathing. Distant dogs bark. Letting a little time pass by again Kabir raises his head, again he stands on his feet. With great difficulty, he begins to walk, again. When darkness abounds and the end seems certain that is when within one a limitlessness is reached. Kabir is surprised that at this juncture he doesn't want to run away or give up on the city or himself. One step at a time he walks, the mind feeling clearer than ever before though the hurt in his body is tearing away into him. Pain is now his only agent for waking up. In the darkness and blur, Kabir puts the dots together, the unseen becomes visible. Of what must have happened in the head of the one who wanted him nailed down. At first what seems to be his imagination soon turns out to be real. In the phosphorescent light ahead of a seedy Bar glowing, Kabir notices the worm-like creature Rancho making his way through hurdles and things. Is it him indeed? Yes, it is Rancho. Kabir's body immediately gets into action. As of now he's resolved to not fail the universe we're holding his hand through this. A mad chase ensues as Rancho knows he is being chased and the one pursuing him will not stop at anything as what is at stake is his innocence. And it is only after proving he is innocent that will he be able to reach out to Sofi or Vijaya and claim his voice and being. He still desires, desires being heard, desires being loved.

They run for a long stretch across the busy roads of Versova, and across a stretch of the beach until Rancho enters an area full of citadels of half-constructed buildings. Cranes bend down like giants looking into mankind like they were worms to be trampled upon, volumes and volumes of cement float all over, and the constant sound of drilling the earth or whirring and grinding and pelting. Kabir is alert, hungry, and light in his head but sharp with the chase. He sees the midget slither into one of the brick-and-mortar assimilations. Kabir follows, he can smell the vapour of Siridevi, like the hiss of a snake, he knows she is around, somewhere close. Kabir climbs the thin, half-made stairs to finally stand in front of what looks like a makeshift apartment, like a homemade for someone inside an elusive structure. He follows and bangs on the door violently.

After some repeated bangs Don opens the door. He guards the door while inside on a silver throne wrapped in ugly red velvet upholstery is seated Siridevi with her legs pulled up to her haunches. She is scared like a child and Rancho barely hides himself in her lap. "I need to talk to her" he signals at Siridevi. Don turns to match eyes with her and a scared Siridevi says yes. As soon as he enters Don shuts the door behind them, Siridevi suddenly throws Rancho off her lap, gets on her knees, and begins to crawl up to Kabir, she pleads with joined hands and as she pleads what shines is her golden tooth. Kabir wriggles at her slimy touch, moves away, and thrashes, "You bitch, you sent me to that godforsaken party, and now that Latika Mehta has died, and I am being called the murderer? What do you think is going on?" Siridevi begins to weep softly, in an apologetic body language groans and moans and pleads her guilt, "I have been hiding from you, I am very, very scared of you, look at my tooth" Siridevi's gold tooth flashes as she cries. Don bends down to hold her up and get her on her feet. As she gets on her feet Kabir who is slightly softened by her tears apologizes, "I could not get a hold of my anger the other day so sorry about that but now you need to help me, please come to the police chowki, all you have to say is on the 19th. Of September you had sent me somewhere or I was with your group wherever you guys were." Don and Siridevi exchange a look. Something inside her is locked now, she gathers herself and says, "Let me think then, let me try and get someone to go and be a witness. Give me a little time?" Saying this as Siridevi turns Kabir pleads, "Siridevi, another day, another time will never, never come. You have to come with me now, right now, I have to get this off my back. Can you understand I am riding on a murder charge?" Siridevi signals Don to step aside, and they exchange a look. Then she steps forward to plead to him hysterically, "Then allow me to dress up? I cannot show the world this face of mine. Can I?" Don nods and signals Kabir to step out, Siridevi giggles vulgarly and asks, "Now don't tell me boy you want me to undress and wear fresh clothes in front of you?" Kabir doesn't wait another second and steps out letting Don close the door on Kabir's face. Kabir stares at the mammoth and vapid construction site, the makeshift space that they have created for Siridevi.

Who would have known she could be here and all because she wanted to hide from him? ...Hide from him? Why? He is not a killer, she knows that. Something does not feel right in his head, and he now impatiently turns and begins to bang on the door, it's thin, its feeble, a few more thrusts and it can give away. Kabir begins to feel more and more scared as there's no response from the other end, no Don's voice threatening him to calm down. After a few seconds, the door falls off on the other side. The walls of the so-called room have collapsed, what stares back at Kabir is the same vapid dark city as before, waiting to coil around his neck and strangulate him. He falls on his knees defeated, tears streaming down his eyes. The dust, the smell of cement and the tears have all become one. His cement-smeared face and helpless rolls of shrieks are absorbed by the indifferent columns of buildings about to come up and become homes to more aspirants, more strugglers in the city.

Once back to Kadam Chawl, as Kabir climbs to his floor wanting to avoid contact with residents in the lift he is visited by her smell. He is never mistaken, it's her. Drawing him to her. He comes drawn to his floor and looks for the source from where it is coming. The door of Tanvi's apartment is wide open, after Alien's death she finds it difficult to keep it closed. As if any time he could come back as if he's gone for a stroll. Kabir knows she's there. Kabir comes up to the door.

Sofi sits holding Tanvi's hand close to her. Her face now has not one but two tapes. One across her nose and the other near her chin. As soon as he makes himself visible Sofi looks up to him. She has tears streaming down her eyes. Tanvi signals Kabir to come close to her while she steps out leaving the space to the damaged lovers. They sit silently hand in hand for a few seconds. Sofi looks up to smile through her tears and scars, "I know you know, who I am and where I come from, and where I will be going. I know that you know. I came to say goodbye." Kabir holds Sofi's hands, tries taking her thin frame in his arms, and explains, "You must stay, please stay back. In this world where everyone wants something out of each other, you came across as the only voice who genuinely wanted to show me the difference between right and wrong. I would have gone into the other stream, lost myself without your voice that pulled me back. You gave me life Sofi, please don't do this to yourself. " Sofi shirks back, this is not the lane where she is going. She gets up and gathers herself fearing sitting a second longer will make things more difficult for her. "Kabir I am glad we met. It has taken me a lot of pain to come this far, I have left no path to look back. Kamal has given me a lot in life, things that I truly wanted and will always want. My lifestyle, my face, they matter to me, and he gives it all. Don't you see they matter to me? Maybe I could launch a career in films, maybe I could sing and tour the world, anything is possible once these scars repair and I reach the Beauty Pageant in China. I have a life waiting for me Kabir. You must make yours now." Without waiting for another second, she races away leaving Kabir empty in his soul and body. Tanvi, standing at a distance a silent spectator to all this knows where Kabir is right now in his heart. She gently comes by to tap him on his shoulder and says, "Such is life, such is this city. Life takes you here, there everywhere! I have been a silent spectator of your life Kabir because I have seen it all. First, the need to prove and then the meaninglessness of it all. But now it's your time to prove yourself and you have to do it, my child? Who else but you? " Kabir is angry, he feels helplessly angry and a rage boiling through his brain. Under his skin flows a river of lava wanting to burst and rip everything apart. This is when Kabir hears a loud sound, of almost a thick, glass pane breaking, it comes from the direction of his house.

Kabir and Tanvi nervously exchange a look, he races away to open his door. The room is semi-dark but a windowpane is broken with the road outside gaping back at Kabir. The intruder did leave it that way. Kabir's tall windows were well locked, and the intruder could have merely slid them open and left. The intention was to create this breakthrough effect. Kabir senses the breath of the being now who had been here about a few seconds back. He races near the windowpane and looks down at a distance. He sees the back of the person racing away towards the rear of the building. He knows that body, that silhouette, he's seen it before. It's Don.

Why was he in Kabir's apartment? To take away, steal what? Or?? Without waiting for another second Kabir begins to pull down everything. Could he plant anything to harm Kabir? And inform the police? Kabir's mind is ticking, for half an hour he pulls down every possible drawer, closet, and corner of his room and stares at the plunder. In the centre of the room, as he stands sweating, his heart thumping, his eyes rest on his father's large photograph. It almost comes alive, as if he were calling out to him. He walks up to it and gently removes it and what comes crashing down is a thick, large candle stand. Kabir stares at it, he has seen it. The whole night comes rushing back to him, the night of vapid sex and drunkenness. It was there, above her bed, he had seen it. At first, it was in Rancho's hand, then he placed it near the bed. He bends to pick it up and notices the blood flecks dried on its edges. It creates an electric wave in him. This is the murder weapon they are throwing at him. Kabir needs to run away now, and the murder weapon is waiting to be found on him. He finds a backpack in the heap of things he's undone. Quickly putting the candlestand into it he races out. Tanvi, who knows he has fire in his body and madness in his brain senses Kabir leaving, she pushes a few currency notes into his hand, and she calls out for him to take care knowing he could tear down the city.

The outside is hot, and blazing. Kabir with the backpack on his back climbs into a vehicle to race towards the same place where he had seen Vimla last. If by magic she could have returned! The construction site like a hollow giant stares back at him, not a trace of anything or anyone. He then again runs to the same cracked, thin lanes of Aram Nagar. While he is almost about to give up unable to trace anything he spots someone. It's that same druggie girl he had seen on his earlier visit, Chamkeeli. A once upon a time dancer is now alive on leftover drugs. Kabir holds her by her hand as she madly looks in the rummage for something, a syringe, a drop of bliss in its emptied barrel. "Where is Vimla? The dance classes? Where did they all go? I know you know; you were with them. Tell me??" She looks at him slyly, she then cheekily smiles and makes a gesture of money, something he must pay. Her quest must meet his. He takes out all the crumpled notes in his wallet and the change too and hands them over to her. As she grabs them she says in spurts, "Red Car..Ref Feraari?? No. 1. She goes riding to heaven in her No. 1 red car!!!" The girl laughs in splits, takes the money gets up and leaves.

Kabir puts the information together in his head. While the outside is normal, usual, grinding away, everything comes to a halt. He saw a red car with number 1 that night in the villa in Madh. While the dwarf was at the swimming pool and before he could show himself Kabir had taken a tour around the fleet of cars, he saw it, he remembers clearly. A red one with the number plate shrieking the single digit 1 looms large, he can't forget it. So, everything is connected to Latika Mehta and how does he now unearth her strings? He looks into his phone quickly for the company name and address. Waves Music, 22/6 Fun Republic, New Link Road. At least that would be a great place to start.

In the blazing afternoon heat, Kabir waits at a distance behind a large pillar in front of the busy, heavily guarded Waves Music building. It's one more large complex with multiple towers in the overcrowded Fun Republic. This is where it all happens. The strugglers move from one door to another requesting one meeting, one sitting, just one chance to say or sing or ardently make an appeal. The Waves Music gate is constantly busy. The guards are very guarded. Until long Kabir waits with no hope. Rohan calls, and Kabir excuses himself saying, "Sir I am this close to not only my alibi but the killer." An alert Rohan sets up the IT guy to locate the location of Kabir.

Finally, the red car pulls up. Its dark window shield conceals everything within. Yes, this was the car he had seen in the villa. There's no movement for a while until one of the doors opens. And in exact coordination a couple of guards emerge from the tower and who emerges from behind them is none other than the owner, be-all and end all of Waves Music, Devang Mehta. Kabir on the other side of the road stares at Don emerging from the car while Devang comes to greet and get into the car. One of the guards who holds a large leather bag gives it to Don. Don peers into it as one would if there were stacks of currencies in it. He then matches his eyes with Vimla and throws it into the car promptly to get into the driving seat. Devang flushes out while Siridevi emerges to be seen with Devang. She brings up the Pallu of her thick gold brocaded saree and rubs it on Devang's head and shoulders. He bends down and takes the blessing while muttering something. He doesn't look pleased, he is in a hurry, and wants to get it done and put this task out of the way. Kabir looks for a vehicle, there will be movement and he will need to race ahead.

As soon as the red car jets off Kabir rushes in a rickshaw urging the driver to keep himself concealed and yet not lose sight of the red car. It's a lazy afternoon, traffic is slow not a hard chase as Kabir might have predicted. The car enters the large gates of Oberoi Springs. Without a word spoken Kabir hands over his card to the rickshaw driver, calls out a pin 043 and plunges towards the basement knowing that's where they will park. Don gets off, and Siridevi gets off, the leather bag with them.

They get into the elevator. Kabir emerges near the elevator door keeping an eye on the numbers above changing. It stops at 14 and stays there. Kabir has no time to waste or wait. He notices a staff exit door of the building. Not waiting for another second, he begins his climb. The climb is making him almost breathless and yet he keeps rising, one step at a time, one level at a time.

But his phone begins to ring amidst this. Something tells him he must pick it up. As he takes it out of his pocket, he is overwhelmed to see his Baba calling. Gasping for breath and with flowing tears Kabir calls out, "Baba?" After a long pause comes a voice from the other end, just as much tear swept. "Yes, it's me, Kabir, I know you did not do it, you can be ambitious, mad about wanting something for yourself, but you cannot kill. I know." Pobon's voice is like a balm to Kabir's parched body and heart. He almost sits on the stairs drowning, victorious in his defeat. His Baba knows it, that is enough, it will be enough, and it doesn't matter what happens now. But almost instinctively Pobon calls out, "You cannot let them defeat you, Kabir, you must stand up. Don't sit down, don't stop, just run, tell them you didn't do it, you are innocent." Kabir nods and the line snaps. He gathers himself and begins to climb again. When he finally arrives at the fourteenth floor panting, sweating through his pores, as he catches his breath he hears "Tamma Tamma Loge" floating in from one of the apartments at the rear end. And he knows that it's where Siridevi and Don are.

Kabir thumps at the door heavily, and then the music stops. Don peers out, Kabir smashes his nose letting him fall on the other side leaving the door ajar. Kabir enters the lit-up apartment where Siridevi is sitting in the centre of it counting money neatly stacked inside the leather bag that Devang Mehta had given her. Kabir comes to the centre of the room, Don by now has gathered himself. He doesn't know whether he should stay back or step out.

Siridevi raises her head and signals Don to leave. As the door shuts Kabir comes close to Siridevi and breathes out aloud, "Why? Why me? Tell me why me? What did I do?" Siridevi dusts off her hands now full of rings of so many coloured stones. Having secured the money stacks neatly on the table back she now gets up and steps out into the attached terrace with the slums beneath looking up at her. She signals Kabir to come where she is standing. "See? See from here, tell me what you see?" Kabir is in no mood to solve puzzles, he remains quiet.

Siridevi carries on, "slum, acres, and acres of slums, long patches of shanties with no sunlight or air entering them, bodies over bodies, all breathing and yet with no feeling of being alive. That is where I come from and that is where I would have died. Raped night after night, raped by drunk neighbours, raped by the police, and raped wherever I went dancing. But now? This is my reality. No one comes to this city to remain a cockroach, you moron. I came here to be on the top and that's where I am, no matter whose shoulder you have to stand on or whom you have to trample under your feet, do it and stand tall!!" With this Siridevi begins to twirl around the terrace basking in her current reality. At a nearby building a shoot is happening, and silver reflectors shimmer in the sunlight. Kabir gets restless, "Siridevi what happened on the 19th night? Who killed whom and why did you put it on me? Just come with me to the police chowki and tell them I didn't do it. Please, I came here only for that" Now even before Kabir can finish his words Siridevi flares up suddenly from nowhere, "But you came here, to this city for what? To become a part of the entertainment industry? I asked you to come the second night for my maalik, why? Why did you not come? All he would do is sit and watch his wife devour you, poor soul, he would have put everything at your feet! Poor thing had to land up killing that bitch wife of his who kept pleading for you, how dare she!"

Though the pieces had started falling together for Kabir it is only now that he wakes up to this fully. So, it was Devang Mehta after all who smashed his wife's head to stop her from bickering or pleading for Kabir the next night after he had come by to the villa on the 17th. Kabir has run out of words; he can't believe all this can make a man flare up enough and kill his wife. Siridevi continues, "Why you..why you? Why Not you? Look what you did to me!" she flashes her gold tooth. Kabir knows the silly games of the rich have cost him what it has cost him, he now pleads to Siridevi, "Whatever has happened has happened dear, now please, please come with me to the police chowki, please help me, I am sorry I hit you that hard, I didn't mean to harm you." Siridevi clicks her tongue and smiles like a devil, "I am not going anywhere, don't you dare imagine I can be of any help to you 'cause I won't. Do you know why society is the way it is? Divided between the very rich and the very poor? The rich only get richer while the poor get poorer. Because that is how we balance it out, you are meant to be where you are, if this city becomes a successful parade of strugglers, then who will throng at the doors of the production houses? Who will run the parlours and gyms? We will always need more. It is only because someone wants it so badly that the other controls it, makes it difficult to attain! And this vicious cycle of wanting? It will never, never change. This is how society is what it is, and this is how there will always be layers, blocks. One on top and one on the bottom. The bottom will never come to the top for they need you to be there, down below. That's what keeps them on the top!"

Siridevi laughs in the midday heat, standing under the sun. Kabir is boiling with rage, all that comes into his range of vision is the neatly arranged stacks of money that Siridevi was counting given to her by Devang. It must have been another transaction, another installment of money she had received for keeping his crime hidden. Kabir suddenly races back to the room, gets the bag, and brings it to the terrace. Now this changes the perspective of Siridevi. She knows something is about to happen that will hit her very hard.

Her entire being is all set to take back the bag from Kabir. She shouts, "What's with the bag? It's my money, give it back to me, how dare you touch it, it's mine..." Kabir knows he has touched her pulse. He now begins to pick the stacks, some currencies come away loose in his hands, "Yours? These are yours? Then why don't you come with me? What did I ask from you? Just to come and say that I am innocent. If you don't come with me, see what I do to your money, here see?" Kabir walks up to the edge of the terrace and begins to throw away the currencies, into thin air. Siridevi can't believe what's going on. Even the shooting crew on the terrace close by stare at this bizarre vision of loose currency notes flying in the city air. Siridevi seeing all her money going now desperate and lost in her head without a thought reaches out to hold on to each of them, "my money my money' she yells and as she tries to hold on to them, she topples over the boundary wall of the terrace. In a flash of a moment even before Kabir can hold on to her thick brocade saree it slips out of his reach and as Siridevi wails and wails for the money her echoes die in the thin city air. The film crew turns on their video camera to capture the whole scene, and in a few seconds, it will be on every social media platform. Kabir falls with his being on the floor, the money flying loose in the air. With Siridevi gone he knows what is lost for him once and for all.

It takes very little time for the police to arrive and arrest him. Through a sea of media, Kabir is taken away, they are pushing, pouring on him, and the police are unable to keep them at bay. They yell, and ask him questions, why, what was his need to kill Latika and, in a way also be the architect of Siridevi's death? Why? Kabir's eyes look lost, he has lost sight of where he is being taken and what he will do or say.

Back in his village, Pobon stares at the large television they have set up in the center, they are looking at Kabir being taken away. Tears flow from Pobon's eyes, he says weeping, "he is not a killer, he is a singer, he cannot kill."

Late that night when Irfaan arrives Rohan gets up with the body language of the accomplished, he calls out to Sule asking for Kabir to be brought in. It's a tiny room, one of the rooms they use for interrogation in the police chowki. They are waiting for orders for Kabir to be taken away to the prison. It's a matter of an hour or so. The nation is bursting and boiling, waiting for justice for Latika Mehta. Suddenly the waves have turned towards the deceased, the rich will be rich and yet aspirational. Their true stories will remain hidden. A Kabir will need to place his head under the guillotine for them to play their games in the dark and let them be at their games.

Rohan tries to shoo off Irfan. "it's all over now Irfan, this case might give you a lot of publicity as you must have come through the ocean of media, but this is it, my friend. It's a matter of a week and he will be hanged. Leave, take my advice. This is not what you want to be a part of, it's risky for all the name and place you claim to have made for yourself!" Irfan seems unmoved, he settles down on a chair calmly.

Rohan has no choice but to settle on a chair on the other side and await Kabir being brought in. After a few seconds, he walks in guarded by two policemen. He settles and looks at Irfan with a flat face. Irfan immediately comes forward to hold his hands and make an attempt to reach Kabir who seems to have gone inside a frozen cellar from where his return might be impossible. "Kabir, you have to speak. You will be taken to court tomorrow. All the names you had taken earlier, Vimla, Don, Rancho, all these people you met and what happened, you must tell it all. I cannot help you if you are not asking for help." A silence persists, Rohan stares at the drama while the old air conditioner continues to whirr in a corner. He waits for Kabir to speak and provokes him too. "Don't you feel the noose closer to your neck Mr. Singer? Speak!!" All that stares back at them is Kabir's silence. Seconds pass by and then minutes. After a while like a sage Kabir gets up and speaks with a voice of finality, 'I will not speak, I have nothing to say, please Sir. I am grateful to you, but this pursuit must stop." Without another word spoken, he walks back to where he came from, a dark deep tunnel. It swallows the Kabir who yearned to sing, who wanted to make a name for himself and become a brand. Irfan is left speechless. Both he and Rohan stare at the boy melting away. They exchange a look, rare is it to find determination and such resolve be visible in the ever-restless youth.

In the depths of the night, Kabir sits in his prison cell waiting. He sings to himself a lullaby his Baba used to sing. Its sound doesn't escape the prison walls and yet someone listens to him, seated in a plush hotel suite, attending to her wounds of the body and soul.

Sofi sits up with a stir, her body telling her he is in pain, her heart wanting to reach out to him. Outside the bedroom in the plush sitting area, Kamal and Dabolkar sit nursing their whiskeys, laughing at the muted media circus on the large, flat TV. He calls out for Sofi; she knows what awaits her on the large sofa. She draws up a line, snorts it up to make herself dizzy, and then pushes herself out into the living room. Kabir's face flashes on the large TV screen, Kamal pulls her down and throws up her silken body suit. He parts her legs hard to dive into her with his drunk, male nakedness. Sofi closes her eyes, but he slaps her hard to keep them open, and turns her stitched chin to the TV. "Look, look at your darling boyfriend while I fuck you." Sofi's eyes stream with tears, and Dabolkar laughs in delight. But inside Sofi's head and heart what abounds is Kabir's tune. His voice, his gaze. The clamoring of sounds and visions burst through Sofi's being. Something is turning, shifting, changing inside her to never go back to where she was. As she lies limp on her side of the bed in the darkness she can reach Kabir, his singing louder than Kamal's abuses.

While the court trials are about to begin in two days and the media is blazing Kabir is again called and told he has a visitor. He knows who it is, he tries to stop himself, but he steps out finally. She sits shrouded in a thick cap and red coloured eyeglasses. Kabir looks away from her, "why have you come? What was the need? It's also not safe for you, go away." Sofi tries to contact Kabir, have his gaze, a look. Not being able to establish contact she looks at a distance, "Why have I come? To have a look at you, before I leave. We are leaving for China finally. The pageant is next week. Kamal also has a lot of clients lined up there. I don't know for how long that stay will be, two months, maybe three. Another country, another city, unknown faces. He will bring me in the open there. By then the scars around the chin and nose will have disappeared. Maybe the beauty pageant will get me a role in a movie, I don't know where you will be then." Kabir finds it more and more difficult to keep himself together. This close to her, her scent, her hot breath makes him want to reach out to her, touch her hair and scars. But it's all gone too far now. He gets up and without turning to her says, "Now that you have seen me, go fulfill your dreams". Kabir walks away, Sofi stares at his back but her sense of parting with him once and for all doesn't seem to have come yet.

Sofi returns to half-packed things all over the Suite. Things she has bought and collected and gathered. Bags, shoes, mascara, and lace bras. She piles them all, parts of her insides not able to gather herself and do it so well as before. Something is giving way while the clock is ticking. In an hour or so Kamal comes and calls out for the service boys to collect everything. As Kamal races ahead Sofi looks on at the Suite. Did she leave anything? Nothing but that carpeted floor, the slab on the terrace, and the wardrobe where she found a touch and smell of love.

The airport is busy, yet something has come to rest. The murderer of Latika Mehta has been arrested and will soon be sentenced to death. Kamal and Sofi float into the lousy business lounge and settle in a corner. Kamal is thrilled and excited with Sofi's face, the way it is all shaped, and her breasts and stomach and legs are all his. She stares at the large TV screen, it's Irfaan. An unusual face on TV as he has never stepped out beyond anything to be of help or kindness. But despite the TV being mute Sofi follows every word, every movement of his mouth. With joined hands, he is appealing, an appeal for Kabir, for someone to step forward and make a confession or be in support of this young man. Something has made Sofi still, very very, still now. She gets up to move in the direction of the lady's washroom. Kamal who was attending to calls from the clinic in China is thrown off by this behavior, he calls out, "But there's a large washroom in our tiny chartered plane Doll, why are you..." Sofi has gone by and it is in her walking away that Kamal notices something has changed, something is different. His lap dog is not under his fold. She is revolting.

Sofi stands still in the large washroom. As she stares at herself in the mirror she is transported to that evening when she was five years old. Her mother had brought her to the music hall in Vile Parle where the organizers had promised a large audience who would listen to Sangeeta Mishra's new songs. Sofi sat in the front row as her mother tuned her vocal cords with the harmonium player and the Sitarist. An hour passed by, and no one came. After a while, the manager came and whispered something in her ears. Sangeeta had paid for the hall, for every single seat for two hours and the show was a free invite. After the manager stepped down one by one the lights started going off in the theatre hall. Her mother had turned stone cold. She got up and came down to ask where the bathroom was. When she wanted to follow Sangeeta stopped her little daughter and said, "Wait here, I am only going for two minutes." The two minutes only ended when a guard woman who had gone in to lock the bathrooms let out a squeal. All that hit Sofi's eyes when she went near the bathroom were streams of her mother's blood. Sofi comes back to the present with a jolt and looks out at the window at a distance bringing in natural light. Thick wedges of glass separate the airport washroom from the world outside. Sofi walks drawn towards the light as if it were calling her.

A few more minutes pass by and then Kamal finds it difficult to hold himself together. He calls for a lady staff and asks her to go and check for Sofi. The woman rushes out in a few seconds asking Kamal to come and check for himself. The window with the thick wedges of glass sheets lay bare. Only a few wedges remain in the bottom and above, streaked with fresh blood. Kamal is devastated and knows she is gone, to never come back to him. He wails aloud, "I am God, if I am God why cannot I control her?"

Rohan and Sule are finishing interviews, and the papers that need to be ready for the trial tomorrow still call for a final round of supervision from Rohan's side. A Havildar comes in saying a woman is asking for Rohan, it's regarding the murder of Latika. Rohan wonders now what this is, he nonetheless asks for the woman to be brought in. Sofi comes and settles on a chair opposite Rohan. Her fingertips are bleeding, her head is throbbing, and she has little time in the world. She finally lets out the words, "Kabir did not kill Latika Mehta on the 19th of September. This is the only truth as I was with him on that night." Rohan can't believe his ears. He gets up to ask in disbelief, "Is this a joke? If you were with him, then why did you not say this earlier? Why are you coming right now? We know it all but have been incapable of helping the boy. It is his need, his desire to be free that could set him free." Sofi remains silent and then after a while takes out a weathered old sheet she had kept folded carefully. "Because of this Sir, here", she gives it to Rohan who is still unable to understand what's going on. As the old photo of Sofi stares at Rohan she explains, "That is me, Sir, that's my case, I jumped parole three years back and I have been all over the place with a changed face. I didn't want to go back to jail, I wanted to be free and live a high life. But I fell in love with Kabir, I cannot enjoy this freedom while a talented singer sits in prison, please set him free, please" Sofi wails aloud. "But I need to meet him one last time Sir only once?" Rohan stares at Sofi unable to believe such a story playing out in front of his eyes. Sule softly speaks unable to stop himself, "Love story hai Sir, kyaa love story hai!" (What a love story this is Sir!). Rohan signals Sule for Sofi to be taken inside.

Sofi and Kabir sit opposite each other. His only question is, "Why? Why did you do it?" Sofi raises her hand to gently touch his face once and for all, "because you deserve to be free more than anyone else. Life is living your desires Kabir not giving them up, go outside, tell the world who the murderer is, and don't let the upper class of society be where they are, someone has to be breaking them down, you be that voice. And sing your songs, sing and charm, and soothe the world, Kabir. I am touched by love now, what will the prison walls do to me or take away from me that I have?" Kabir is overwhelmed.

They hug, and their time is finally up. Kabir walks under the open sky with the media gathered to only hear from him. Sofi walks into her tunnel of oblivion holding the touch of love close to herself.

Irfan comes across to hug him, and his father does. Rohan and his team race to the Waves Music building. Don flees into some remote corner of the city. And by the time Rohan and his team reach the level where Devang thrives, he takes out his pistol and kills himself. The gap between him and the law is now taken care of by death. Siridevi's plush and empty flat stares out at the city.

Kabir walks back with Pobon to the same red earth of Dhulishor he had left years back. He bows to its soil and kisses it. Its smell has become one with the soft smells of Sofi's body that never leaves his side. The earth crackles to rain love on him. After the showers have poured out, and the earth is soft and fertile again Kabir sets up his phone and strings up his guitar. Looking up at the wide, abounding sky standing on the very earth that birthed him he sings his song to the world. The band of Bauls strum their Dotaara in unison. Pobon cries as he hears Kabir's tune of desire and love reach out and call the Gods above, in it he sees God.

Epilogue

Three years have passed by. Sofi does not know what date or time it is, they come up and say her time is up. She has hardened in these years of hard work, remembered love and told herself she will have a life ahead of her where she doesn't know what to do. On the prison radio, they sometimes play his songs. Earthy, vibrant, rocking from one corner of the earth to another. They return her the clothes she came in, the tiny jewels that were on her. As she signs the papers and takes her things the aged jailor Rehman who has seen her all these years asks, "What will you do now child? Where will you go?" Sofi signs her name Vijaya Mishra and smiles at the jailor, thinks, and says, "I wish I knew Sir, to have come this far was a journey in itself. Now once I am out let me see what I do with my life."

Sofi walks past the cool courtyard of the prison. As she nears the large gate of the prison, she hears loud sounds rolling in from the outside, as if there were a mob or a gathering in an uproar. Her heart trembles not knowing what awaits her there. Oblivious to reality she finally comes and stands in front of the thick prison door waiting for it to open. Her heart is thumping today, aloud, something tells her she feels like the first time she met Kabir. The prison door opens, and the heat and cheer of the outside hit her in her stomach like she were to pass out. She can see a sea of heads, flashes, cameras, and from amidst them a leaner, slightly mature Kabir walking up to her. She tells herself it's a surprise, but her heart knows it's him, he has come for her. He stands in front of her and gently bows, Sofi holds him in her arms and cries. The crowd cheers and calls out their names. A story is formed. A love story here and now begins.

THE BEGINNING

www.ingramcontent.com/pod-product-compliance
Lightning Source LLC
LaVergne TN
LVHW041948070526
838199LV00051BA/2950